ME AND MARVIN GARDENS

AMY SARIG KING

SCHOLASTIC INC.

ISBN 978-1-338-21622-6

Arthur A. Levine Books hardcover edition published by Arthur A. Levine Books, an imprint
of Scholastic Inc., February 2017

12 11 10 9 8 7 6 5 4 3 2 1   18 19 20 21 22 23

Printed in the U.S.A.   40

First Scholastic paperback printing, January 2018

Book design by Maeve Norton and Abby Denning
Map styling and illustrations by Maeve Norton

FOR L.B.K. AND G.E.K.,
MY CREEK GIRLS

*The real voyage of discovery consists
not in seeking new landscapes
but in having new eyes.*

— MARCEL PROUST

CHAPTER 1

NOSEBLEEDS & MOSQUITOES

There were mosquitoes. There were always mosquitoes at Devlin Creek this time of year. Every time I went inside I had twenty more bites than I had the last time, and Mom made a noise as if it was my fault. As if I created mosquitoes.

There was a bloody nose. It wasn't my first. I didn't have any tissues or napkins and I was in a good T-shirt so I lay on my front with my head out over the bank and let the blood drip into the creek. I wondered if the fish would smell it or taste it or breathe it. I knew by then that nosebleeds only lasted so long. I'd learned not to pinch my nose or tilt my head back six months ago. You just had to let it bleed until it was done.

Most people got nosebleeds because something happened. Like maybe they got hit with a baseball or walked into a door. I got nosebleeds for no reason.

Or there was a reason.

I just didn't like to talk about it.

I reached down and picked out a plastic shopping bag that was floating downstream and put it on the bank next to me. This was my job. This was my creek. It was named after my family. One hundred years ago, the Devlins owned everything around here. Mostly fields, and the old original farmstead—a big red stone house and a barn and a few sheds. Now there were only our small farmhouse and one tiny field left. I couldn't really call it a field. It was more like a wild patch with the creek running through it and a small area of woods. We didn't farm it because we weren't farmers anymore. My dad was a manager of an electronics store. My mom worked in a warehouse putting items in boxes so people didn't have to leave their house to buy things.

One hundred years ago, things were different. World War I was raging. Nobody flew in airplanes for vacation. One hundred years ago, a shark attacked a bunch of people at the New Jersey seashore and there was a polio epidemic. One hundred years ago, somebody invented the light switch.

I bet boys still had turf wars one hundred years ago. I bet people got punched in the nose then too. Territory and violence are pretty much a million years old.

•••

I grew up in the middle of a cornfield. It wasn't our field anymore, but it was Devlin dirt—worked and cared for by my family's sweat for more than a century. The land was so important to my mother's family that for two generations, daughters

2

chose to keep the family name — Devlin — and when they had children, they gave it to us, too, instead of our fathers' boring last names. The name and the land belonged together, even though we didn't own the land anymore. I never thought about the new owner. It was Devlin dirt. That's all I knew. The whole cornfield was my turf. I ran in it, bicycled through it, played in it, and sometimes I'd just walk and let the leaves hit me in the face because nothing made me smell more like me than the smell of a walk in the cornfield. Now, my turf ended where the corn used to be, just outside our wild patch. Tommy and his new friends had the woods. I got to keep Devlin Creek.

Mom said we should feel lucky we had anything at all because her grandfather drank 175 acres of Devlin land.

I remember when she said it to me the first time. I said, "How did he drink land?"

She never explained, but my sister, Bernadette, told me later that night.

"Mom's grandfather was a drunk."

"He was *drunk*?" I figured he had to be drunk to drink dirt.

"No. He was a drinker. You know," she said. "He had a *problem*."

She could tell I still didn't understand. I was probably seven. I don't think most seven-year-olds understand how these two things can relate. A drunk great-grandfather still didn't explain how 175 acres of land wasn't ours anymore.

"He lost the land because he spent all his money at the bar, get it?" she said. "Like money he didn't even have — he used it to buy more drinks?" I nodded. She smiled. I liked Bernadette. She helped me with my homework and with questions I couldn't ask Mom or Dad, and she was nice to me. I didn't think a lot of older sisters were nice. I knew Tommy's wasn't.

My nosebleed slowed down, so I sat up and faced the tree line between our wild patch and the old cornfield. On the other side of the tree line, there were bulldozers, earth diggers, and dump trucks. That's what happened when all your great-grandfather's land is sold and sold again and sold again. Bulldozers. My road, Gilbrand Road, used to have just our house and Tommy's long driveway to his house for a mile stretch. Now there were four housing developments and a gas station. And bulldozers. And traffic. And neighbors. And turf wars.

Mosquitoes don't have turf wars. Mosquitoes just want to drink blood. They don't have a *problem*. It's the way they are. The females are the only ones that drink blood. Did you know that? Males drink nectar and sweet stuff like that. I learned this in science class — my favorite class — from Ms. G, my favorite teacher. She knew everything and made science exciting.

I watched closely as a mosquito landed right on my bony knee-cap. I didn't think she could get blood from there, but she stuck her proboscis in and started to fill up with my blood. She got fatter and fatter as I watched. Tommy used to wait until a mosquito got full and then slap it dead so the blood would spatter all over his arm or whatever.

Maybe it wasn't normal for a kid to watch a mosquito drink blood from his own kneecap and not want to slap it. Maybe it wasn't normal to care so much about land that was never really

4

mine but would have been if my great-grandfather didn't have a *problem*. Maybe I was weird for collecting trash that flowed down from upstream or for owning a guide to animal tracks so I could identify what animals came to drink at the creek. Maybe no one cared about Devlin Creek anymore. But I did. I was part of it as much as it was part of me, because now my blood was running through its veins.

I heard Bernadette's activity bus drop her off at the end of our driveway and realized it was time for dinner. I splashed cold creek water on my face to erase any sign of my nosebleed. The noise of this startled something in the brush between the creek and the tree line. Probably a stray cat or something. It was too early for frogs that big. Turtles were slower. It sounded bigger than a cat, though.

I could see its eyes through the high grass. It was staring at me and I was staring at it. It wasn't a cat. It was taller. But it wasn't a dog either. The eyes were farther apart than any animal that had ever come to the creek before. As we stared at each other, I felt like it was just as curious about me as I was about it.

Then Mom rang the bell for dinner and I stood up and it scurried into the creek and downstream. From the back it looked like an armadillo. We don't have armadillos in Pennsylvania. I figured it was maybe just a wet dog, but I knew deep down it wasn't one.

CHAPTER 2

APPLE SAUSAGE & MASHED POTATOES

There were dinner bells. This bell was the Devlin Bell. One hundred years ago, the bell called family and farmhands spread over 175 acres in for meals. Forty years ago, it called Mom and her brothers and sister in from forty acres they rented from the new owner. Now, we had only three acres and Mom could just yell my name and I'd hear her, but she used the bell anyway. It was the only time she came outside anymore when she wasn't getting into her car to go to work.

It was Monday. Bernadette was still in her softball practice clothes. She was a varsity freshman, which meant that she was good enough to play varsity even though she was only a fourteen-year-old ninth grader.

"Can you mash these for me?" Mom asked, and Bernadette washed her hands and mashed a pot of potatoes.

I set the table because that was my job. I folded the square paper napkins into triangles and placed a fork on top to the left of the plate. Knives and spoons on the right. We never used the spoons but I had to put them out anyway. I kept thinking about the animal at the creek. It really didn't look like a dog.

"Drinks, Obe."

When Mom called me by my nickname, she used one syllable. Obe, like *lobe* without the *L*. But it was spelled the same as my real name, Obe, which was what you might say if a yellow jacket wasp showed up. *Oh! Bee!* Obe. A weird name, maybe, but I lucked out compared to Bernadette, because the only way to shorten her name is *Bernie* and that was a guy's name . . . which is why she wanted everyone to call her Bernadette.

Anyway, most kids thought I was named after Obi-Wan Kenobi from *Star Wars* and I let them believe it. In real life, I was named after my granduncle—the son of the man who drank all the Devlin land except for our house and our little wild patch. I liked to believe that Obe meant "Son of a man who drank dirt" but really it had something to do with God or my having a big heart or something.

At dinner Dad was cranky and talked about how stupid people . were about electronics. Stuff like: *He returned the computer because the Internet didn't work and he doesn't even have Internet service! . . . Claimed it came from the factory with honey in the DVD player and the sticky kid was standing right there! . . . Who puts a phone in the microwave to dry it?*

I climbed inside my plate of dinner and ate too fast. I didn't have anything to say about electronics. I was too busy thinking about the animal. I could still see it scurrying away in my head.

Bernadette talked about softball because Mom and Dad asked her how practice went. While she talked, I thought about my pocket guide to animal tracks and tried to remember where I put it. The last place I saw it was in my room.

Mom turned to me and said, "Obe, slow down."

I slowed down but I kept thinking about the animal and how it wasn't a dog or a cat or a possum or anything else I ever saw.

"How'd you do on your math test today?"

"Great."

"I'm sure you did great," Dad said.

"It was easy," I said. I felt myself get nervous as I said it, though. I probably didn't do so great.

I cut a piece of apple sausage, scooped up mashed potatoes, and then rolled it in my corn and stuffed it in my mouth before anyone could ask anything else.

Too late. Dad said, "Are you trying out for summer baseball this weekend?"

I shook my head no.

"But you're so good at it!" Mom said.

Bernadette said something but I couldn't hear her over the sound of my own brain trying to come up with an excuse for not joining summer baseball. I readied the next bite, but before I could put it into my mouth, Dad reached over and touched my forearm, right on a mosquito bite, which made it itch.

"So what if Tommy What's-His-Face gave you a hard time, right? You're young. He could be your friend next week again. Things change a lot when you're young. Blah blah blah blah blah blah. Blah blah? I mean, blah blah blah blah and blah blah were blah blah blah . . . So why don't you just think about it?"

My plate was empty. The sun hadn't set yet. We ate early on Mondays because Mom worked the six-to-midnight shift at the warehouse.

"I'm going to go clean up the creek," I said.

"Manners," Mom said.

I said, "May I please be excused? I'd like to go clean up the creek."

Mom nodded and smiled. Dad said, "You spend too much time cleaning up after people."

Bernadette said, "I think it's nice. He wants to help the environment."

Dad laughed and *blahed* out a few sentences about what he thought about the environment. Something about how recycling is a joke *blah blah blah*. Something about how if it still snows in winter *blah blah blah*, the world wasn't getting any hotter.

I don't know what sixth grade was like thirty years ago when Dad was there, but I bet Ms. G could teach him a thing or two.

CHAPTER 3

HOUSE SEEDS & MY LIVER

There was a mess. On a large scale, it was a mess of *New Spacious Homes!* where my field used to be. On a smaller scale, there was a creek full of throwaway things humans never think twice about. On an even smaller scale, there was my bedroom.

My room was too apocalyptic to find my animal track guide. I put on a sweatshirt, stuffed one pocket with a plastic shopping bag for trash and the other with my flashlight so I could look for tracks, and tissues just in case, and walked through the wild patch toward the creek.

Upstream were two finished housing developments and across the tree line was a flattened dirt wasteland scattered with construction equipment that looked like monsters in the falling light. The developer bought the last of the Devlin fields six months ago and planted more house seeds. Soon, more houses would grow.

Downstream, it didn't take long before the creek emptied into the Schuylkill River. Down in Philadelphia, the Schuylkill emptied into the Delaware River, which eventually emptied into the Delaware Bay, which eventually led you to the Atlantic Ocean.

So, the ocean started here, at Devlin Creek. That's how I saw it.

The excavator and bulldozer guys upstream took their breaks by the creek. I watched them sometimes during summer. They cursed a lot. Some of them smoked and threw their cigarette butts into the water. They left their lunch trash on the bank — fast-food bags, water bottles, supersized drink cups, sometimes even a beer can. The workmen didn't seem to understand rain or nature. If they did, they'd know that their Big Mac containers would eventually end up downstream — maybe in the Atlantic Ocean. If I did my job right, their Big Mac containers ended up in my trash bag.

There were no trash cans where they worked, just a landscape of dirt that they moved and dug and moved again. Some days there were huge holes that would one day be some kid's basement rec room. One hundred years ago, people dug basements by hand and it took a long time. Now, the machines could dig one in an hour or two.

I went to the creek bank, stepping slowly and looking down for tracks. All I saw were my own footprints from before dinner. I crossed the creek on the bridge I made from a small tree trunk the workmen bulldozed. I'd dragged it from a pile a year ago. It was just wide enough — I'd only fallen off twice.

On the far bank of the creek there were tracks. I shone my flashlight down and saw domestic cat tracks first — easy to spot.

Closer to the tree line there were opossum tracks. Opossums have really weird feet. I didn't see any skunk tracks. Not even with my flashlight. Strange, because skunks loved Devlin Creek. Raccoons too, but I didn't see any raccoon tracks either.

Something moved in the brush about ten feet from me and I stood still. I turned my head slowly and whatever it was stopped moving. I figured it was the not-a-dog I saw before dinner. I aimed my flashlight in the direction of the rustling sound. No more sound. There was sound in the distance. It was Tommy and his friends playing war in the woods. On their turf.

I never liked playing war anyway.

I crossed back over the bridge and sat in my favorite spot and looked around. I found a rock — a small piece of quartz — and I put it in my pocket for Annie Bell, who lived in *Phase One*, which was the first development they'd built on the old Devlin land.

My nose felt a familiar feeling. It was just like snot but something was warmer about it when it was blood. I dug into my sweatshirt pocket and found the lump of tissues and put them to my nose. I kept shining my flashlight around the bank. And then I saw the track. I was sitting right next to it.

If I was Bernadette, I would have just taken out my phone and snapped a picture of it, but I was eleven so I didn't have a phone or even a decent camera. I tried to take a mental picture.

It had toes and a central pad, but also had a hoofed edge. It was part dog and part pig or something. It made no sense, this track. I tried to picture the foot that could have made it. I looked for others, and when there were no others, I figured someone must have been playing a joke on me. Tommy knew about my pocket guide to animal tracks. He was with me when I found my first beaver track downstream. That was the first day he called me *Creek Boy.*

CREWAHARKKKLTKELTH!

The noise made the hair on my arms and legs stand straight up. Maybe the hair everywhere. My heart beat fast and I thought it was Tommy and his friends because I didn't believe stories about monsters or ghosts. But it wasn't Tommy.

The animal was five feet from me, half in the creek, half on the bank.

It was definitely not a dog.

It was definitely not any animal I ever read about in Ms. G's class or in any other class or in any book.

All I could see in the fading light was its outline and its outline didn't make any sense. It looked like a pig, I guess, but lower to the ground. It had big teeth, but I thought maybe I was imagining how big. It was munching on a pint-sized plastic water bottle and the sound was worse than bulldozers backing up at seven in the morning. Worse than those tree-eating machines that spit out mulch.

CREWAHARKKKLTKELTH! CREWAHARKKKLTKELTH!

The animal wasn't scared of me. It just sat there munching, making this deafening noise. Then, with one push of its paw/ hoof, it shoved the rest of the plastic bottle into its mouth and swallowed.

Wild animals don't eat plastic.

What was this thing?

I could still hear Tommy and his friends playing. They sounded farther away now. I couldn't tell how long I'd been out there or if it was more light than dark or if I had homework that night or anything. I thought I was in shock. I'd never been in shock, but I thought I was in it. I was sweating and cold at the same time.

The animal/creature/monster/thing started to move toward me. It wasn't careful or shy. It came full speed up the bank, loping toward me, and I opened my mouth to scream because I just knew I was going to be the next thing it chewed and my death would be horribly loud and lonely. Then I thought it would be nice to die by Devlin Creek. I thought a hundred other things, but none of them were fully formed.

The thing came straight for my torso and opened its jaws.

I was frozen. I looked at the sky and still couldn't tell if it was more dark than light. I couldn't really see the thing as it attacked me. *Maybe I'm blacking out. Maybe it already bit me and sucked out my liver or something.*

Then, the noise.

It was different this time, like he was using a different kind of teeth to eat my liver. Bernadette told me once about out-of-body experiences. It's when something bad is happening and your brain or your soul or whatever leaves your body and can watch what's going on from above. I couldn't tell if that's what I was having. Maybe when a weird animal started eating your liver, this sort of confusion was normal.

I felt it pressing against my side.

14

When I looked down, there was blood all over my sweatshirt and the animal was tugging something from my insides. I didn't feel anything but pressure — the way it had felt when the dentist numbed my tooth before he filled my one cavity that Mom would never let me live down.

Finally, the animal pulled away. It had yanked my plastic bag out of my pocket. Once it got the bag, it sat down right next to me like it was some sort of Labrador retriever. No tail. Just a nub. But it wagged all the same.

While it munched on the bag, I felt my side and I was pretty sure I still had my liver. I remembered where the blood was coming from and found the wad of tissues I'd dropped by my side.

I didn't hear Tommy anymore. It was definitely more dark than light.

I had no idea where my flashlight was. I felt around but it wasn't on the creek bank and it wasn't in my pockets.

The animal nudged me. I reached out and touched it.

It was totally, unquestionably, certainly, worryingly *not* a dog.

CHAPTER 4

BIGFOOT & MONOPOLY

There was my liver—exactly where it was supposed to be. There were tissues cupped around the base of my nose. There was a creature who looked up at me with kind eyes and I wanted to pet it because it seemed to need it. I don't know how to explain it. By the time the whole liver confusion was over, we both needed affection.

It was like petting algae. Or snot. Sounds gross, but it was more like that goo you get in a jar instead of real snot. It was a good kind of snot. Like Jell-O. Either way, I petted the thing and it was warm and I didn't look at it at first. I just petted it like it was a dog because I wanted it to be a dog because I'd never had a dog.

The thing made a sucking noise as it ate my trash bag, but

underneath it sounded like purring. I looked down. In the low light I could only see its snout. Not quite like a pig—more wild than that, and then cute like a dog on the end. It was too big for a cat, too small for a Labrador retriever. It was a mystery of twenty questions.

Animal, vegetable, or mineral? Animal.

Is it a mammal? I think so.

Is it bigger than a bread box? Bigger.

That's all I had. I didn't think anyone had ever tried to describe a creature like this, and I didn't think anyone liked to admit they'd seen an animal that no one ever saw before. Especially an animal that seemed to eat plastic.

Look at all those people who believed in Bigfoot. Everyone thought they were crazy. People have seen him, have taken pictures of huge Bigfoot tracks. People have recorded actual accounts of seeing Bigfoot, and it was no different than when someone said they saw a UFO.

Wacko. Crazy. Loony. That's what they were.

But here I was petting a slimy not-dog and I didn't think I was crazy at all.

It was past dark. Dad was going to kill me for several reasons. My sweatshirt was covered in blood. I hadn't done well on my math test and I'd lied about it. He didn't know that yet. Only Bernadette knew that the reason I hated math was because of the math teacher, Mr. Salt, who we called Mr. Mustache on account of his dumb mustache, who'd hated Bernadette and now hated me. Dad didn't know that part and wouldn't care. He would just look at my grades and get mad the same as he looked at my not trying out for summer baseball and got mad.

The animal stayed sitting next to me after it ate the bag because it seemed to think it found a friend. Maybe it had. I hoped I'd see it the next day. Maybe we could hang out after school because I didn't have anyone to hang with after school. Annie Bell wasn't allowed to leave her yard once she got off the bus. The only friend I had before that was the reason I always had nosebleeds.

I kept petting the animal until I was sure it was all dark and no light. I patted its gooey head and got up, and when I turned around to walk through the wild patch toward home, it followed me.

I said, "No. You have to stay here. Stay."

Because weird creatures no one ever saw before didn't understand human language, it kept following me. I bet Bigfoot didn't understand humans either.

So I ran.

It let out some sort of shallow cry and I ignored it because which is better? Getting in trouble for all the real rules I'd broken or getting in trouble for bringing home a weird animal? Even when I brought cute animals home, it was never a good idea.

I stood outside the back door, and I removed my sweatshirt and balled it in my arms, bloody side in. I decided to do the burst-through-the-door entrance as if I'd sprinted in an effort to get home on time. I even jogged in place outside the back door for a while so I'd be out of breath.

When I opened the door and ran in saying *"Sorry I'm late but I didn't notice it was getting that dark and I fell in the mud so I have to go rinse out this sweatshirt!"* no one was there to hear me.

I went upstairs to my room. Mom and Dad's bedroom door was closed. Bernadette's bedroom door was closed and she was listening to her old-people music. She was into the 1960s. She said stuff like *groovy* and owned a pair of suede-tassel moccasins. She said she was a flower child. Creek Boy and Flower Child. That was us.

I closed my bedroom door, dropped the bloody sweatshirt on the floor, and started looking for my animal track guide. It wasn't under any of my clothes. It wasn't in any of my overstuffed drawers. It wasn't in my closet. Wasn't on my nightstand. Wasn't in the two stacks of books next to the bookshelf.

I knew what was under my bed. Everything. Everything was under my bed. Probably the cool glow-in-the-dark rattlesnake T-shirt my aunt sent me from Arizona. Probably my favorite pair of jeans from last year. A random flip-flop I couldn't find all last summer. Without my flashlight there was very little chance of me finding anything under my bed.

I needed the book, though.

So I started on the most obvious side — right by my nightstand — and I used my hand to search. I moved around the perimeter and finally I felt it. Small, spiral bound, and the binding was caught on something so I couldn't pull it out without dragging the other thing with it.

The missing yellow sock. Mom would be so happy I found it.

I sat on the floor and paged through the book's tabs: HOOF, RODENT, RABBIT, DOG, CAT, WEASEL, RACCOON, BEAR, BIRDS. From what I remembered seeing, the closest hoof I could find was a peccary and that made no sense because we didn't have peccaries in Pennsylvania. But the hoof part was blocky, and so was the peccary's. The top was like a wolf. Not a coyote, which did show up around here sometimes. But I remembered the toes being spread out more. Definitely more wolf than coyote or fox. Maybe a big weasel . . . but with half a hoof.

I went downstairs to the computer. Mom and Dad didn't let us have computers in our rooms because Dad thought the Internet was dangerous and *blah blah blah.* I didn't know where to start. *Animals that eat plastic* seemed good.

Mealworms and barnacles can eat plastic. I knew I hadn't been petting a mealworm or a barnacle by the creek, though. Goats and squirrels and all sorts of animals eat a little plastic but not for food, not the way that creature had been eating my bag. There weren't any more search results that matched, just articles about what to do if your dog accidentally eats a plastic bag.

I searched *Animals with gooey skin.* I found an article about a new species of frog and another one about naked mole rats. No articles mentioned larger, not-a-dog animals that ate plastic.

I'd have to make sure the next day in daylight, but I pretty much knew right then that I'd discovered a brand-new animal. I thought about who I could tell but there wasn't anyone. A few months ago, I'd have told Tommy — I'd have called him right then — but now I couldn't tell Tommy. Everyone in my family was too busy or wouldn't believe me. Maybe I shouldn't tell anybody. People would think I was crazy. People might haul the animal away and do experiments on it or something. The best thing to do for now was to stay quiet until I knew more. And I couldn't wait to know more.

CHAPTER 5

DIRT & SHOVELS

There were piles of dirt. There were always piles of dirt. It wasn't the right color dirt. When the farmer plowed the cornfield all those years before, the dirt was red and brown. This dirt was deep dirt. It was yellowish-brown and gray. It had rocks in it. This was basement dirt. When I climbed the piles and stood on top, I used to think: *I am standing on top of your basement even though your basement is in your basement.*

Sounds stupid, but it worked for me.

During *Phase One*, which started the summer between third and fourth grades, they built the main road that would link Gilbrand Road and all the development phases together one day. The road was called Orchard Way. It cut the field in half and was close to my house even though back then, the houses wouldn't be close to my house yet. I should really draw you a map.

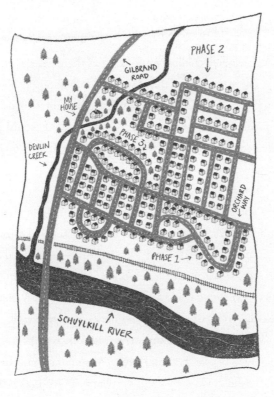

During *Phase One* I had this idea that I'd somehow get into the basements of all the houses and bury something of mine in there. Something special. Something Devlin. I was like a dog peeing on trees to mark territory. Someone could build a house, buy it, move in, customize the kitchen, the deck, the front porch. But underneath it all would be me and my family. They'd never even know.

Of course this idea didn't work out because that's not how basements are built. Dirt basement holes are too deep to get out of if you jump into them. Tommy and I learned this on the first one. Only I jumped in and he had to run home and get some rope to get me out. I think it was hitting us then. They were taking our field. There wasn't anything we could do about it. Nothing.

During *Phase One* we used to climb the dirt piles together. We used to get in trouble because the nuggets of soil would get into our socks and onto our feet and our sneakers turned brown and yellow inside and out.

When Tommy and I climbed those piles of dirt, we'd rotate clockwise and look at what had become of our field. Our corn-filled paradise. Our meeting place. The things we'd named. *The House*—which was really the two-hundred-year-old oak tree. *The Rosebush*, which wasn't a rosebush at all but a strange weed the farmer never managed to kill or didn't want to. When it was still a field, we'd meet at these landmarks and then walk through the rows of corn to the school playground in summer. Or we'd start a game of tag or hide-and-seek. You might think hide-and-seek in a cornfield was easy but it was hard. The secret is to count to one hundred. That gives the corn a while to settle after you move through it.

Anyway, they fill basements with cement right after they dig them. That's what they do most of the time. Still, the open house, the first house they built on Orchard Way, had my favorite Tonka truck under it. I was eight then. Tonka trucks were a big deal. Throughout the next school year Tommy and I would bury things anywhere we could in each new lot. Under the preformed front steps. Under the back deck. Next to the mailbox. Every single house in *Phase One* had something of mine buried there. After *Phase One* was built, they started all over again on *Phase Two*. The farmer who'd planted corn all those years had only one-third of his original field left now. I had this idea that the owner wouldn't sell the whole field—that he'd stop at *Phase Two*.

Phase Two was closer to my house, and right on the edge of Tommy's backyard. He'd have neighbors all around him by the following summer. He got really angry. He wanted to do bad things to the construction equipment. But he only talked about sabotage and never did anything. Instead, we stood on the piles of dirt and we said nothing to each other. We stopped watching them dig. We still buried things, but we did it with a heavy feeling in our stomachs. We played only in the last bit of nature that was left—the last twenty acres between my house and the river.

Now, *Phase Two* was finished and all the construction equipment moved to *Phase Three*, which were those final twenty acres. The farmer hadn't been making that much money and the owner couldn't refuse the developer's deal. Now, Tommy wasn't my friend anymore. Now, standing on those dirt piles was worse. So much worse. Even when he was mad, Tommy had cracked the jokes I needed to handle what was happening during *Phase One* and *Phase Two*.

Now, I was missing the only person in the world who understood what this meant—this *Phasing* of our turf.

Maybe not the *only* person.

During *Phase One*, I watched my mother cry for weeks. She couldn't wake up without being so angry at the bulldozers that she'd yell at them, knowing they couldn't hear her. She yelled at all of them. The tree fellers. The bark mulch makers. The surveyors. The dump trucks. The cement trucks. The asphalt trucks. The steamrollers. The builders. The piles of dirt. Maybe that's what made me so sad. Knowing she was the last one to care. She was the last Devlin to hear her mother's stories about planting the trees along Gilbrand Road that the chain saws cut down. She was the last one who knew the secrets of her grandfather, my great-grandfather, who drank dirt.

She didn't know it, but sometimes when I buried things, they were her things. A trinket from a trip she took to Washington, DC, when she was in high school that she'd gifted to me. A favorite pair of slippers she threw out when they got too ratty. A sport wristwatch she gave me because the band was too small for her wrist and she hated the sound of the alarm.

I'd buried those things. I had a map so I knew what was where. It was like a treasure map, except I wasn't burying treasure. I was burying the last of our family, where one hundred years ago, the Devlin erosion had begun.

CHAPTER 6

ONE HUNDRED YEARS AGO

One hundred years ago, my great-grandmother wrote things down inside the Farmer's Almanacs Mom still keeps on the bookshelf. My great-grandfather plowed this field, *Phase Three*, on March 23, 1916. He didn't own a tractor yet, so he worked the land with two workhorses and a walking plow. The day before, the last emperor of China abdicated his throne. The day after, a German submarine planted two torpedoes in a French passenger ferry in the English Channel, killing more than fifty people. By this time, my great-grandfather was drinking at Hannah's Bar every night, and that year he decided he was going to farm tomatoes. A risk, but worth it if it worked out. It didn't work out. There were no savings. The bank let him mortgage twenty acres. This was the beginning.

CHAPTER 7

JAIL & PLASTIC

There was greed. There had always been greed. Greed pretty much ruined everything fun and good in the world. Maybe that's a negative attitude. But my science teacher, Ms. G, says the reason we have so much pollution is because of greed. Companies make more money when they don't follow the rules. Everybody wants bigger and better things all the time. Everyone wants to move up in the world, even if it means they have to hurt things to get there. Just like turf wars. Just like Monopoly.

Dad came into the study where I was sitting at the computer, still staring at a picture of a naked mole rat and thinking about the animal at the creek.

He said, "Whatcha doing?"

I was processing ten things at a time. I was remembering what the animal's hoof/paw looked like when it shoved that bottle into its mouth. It had fingers. Not fingers like mine, but pads and claws. I said, "Nothing."

"Feel like a game of speed Monopoly?"

"It's a school night. I was going to read my book," I said, holding up my animal track guide. I didn't mention my math homework.

"You've already read it a million times, right? We should do something fun."

Dad had recently become addicted to Monopoly, and this was a chance to get out of math homework. I said yes. Who else had a dad who wanted to play a board game on school nights? We went up to drag Bernadette into the game.

When she opened her door, I looked inside and saw all the order that my room didn't have. Her bed was made, for starters. Her schoolbooks were spread out on her bed as if she was really studying when I knew she was probably texting her friends the whole time. She and Dad headed down the steps to the kitchen/Monopoly table.

I told them I'd be down in a minute and went to get my sweatshirt, which was still balled up and bloody on my bedroom floor. I knew all about how to wash blood out of clothing. Mom had to teach me on that first day of the turf war. I filled the bathroom sink with cold water and put the sweatshirt in and squeezed it a lot to get the blood out. The water turned pink. I rinsed it again until there was no more pink and then left it there to soak.

In the past six months, I'd had to do this probably twenty times.

Playing Monopoly with Dad was kind of fun, but pointless. Bernadette knew this as much as I did. It wasn't so much that he was smart, but that he was ruthless. Also, I always thought he stole money from the bank because he was the banker. He'd move his hand fast over the colorful bills and he always had more than he should. When Bernadette and I played Monopoly by ourselves, I built houses and hotels on my properties, but never with Dad. With Dad, I just hoarded properties and said it was my personal choice not to build anything on them. It drove him crazy.

I couldn't stop thinking about the animal. And my flashlight. I hoped I didn't drop it in the creek. I hoped the animal didn't eat metal too. The flashlight was a birthday present and a real Maglite — the small kind — and I took it everywhere with me.

"You owe me four hundred and fifty dollars," Dad said.

One hundred years ago, Monopoly existed but it was called something else. A woman named Lizzie something invented it in 1903 to teach people about the evils of land development by small monopolies and something about taxes. I wasn't really sure what a monopoly was, but I could see the evils Lizzie something wanted people to see when I watched Dad hold his hand out to me for $450 in rent . . . which he knew I didn't have.

Bernadette offered to loan me a hundred bucks, but Dad wouldn't allow it. I mortgaged a few of my properties so I could scrounge up enough money to pay him, and when it was my turn, I landed on the GO DIRECTLY TO JAIL space and happily went to jail. At least I'd be free of debt for three turns.

Dad said to me, "You know I have to pay for trash removal and recycling."

Bernadette rolled a four and landed on St. Charles Place, which she owned, so she said, "Phew!"

Dad said, "I don't like you bringing home all that trash from the creek and my having to pay for it."

"They don't charge you by the pound, do they?" I asked.

"That's not the point," he said. "It's not our trash."

"All trash is our trash," I said. "I mean, if you think of it a certain way."

I rolled and didn't roll doubles so I had to stay in jail. Dad rolled and landed on a railroad and had to pay me fifty bucks.

"I don't want you bringing home trash anymore."

"It's our land, Dad. It's our creek. It's our trash."

"I didn't put it there."

Bernadette rolled her eyes and said, "But if no one picks it up, then it stays there."

"Exactly," Dad said.

I imagined what Ms. G would say to him then. I tried to come up with something smart with facts and numbers and interesting side stories.

Ms. G had a framed newspaper article on her classroom wall about an experiment she did back in the 1980s. She asked her students to start collecting the pull tabs from the tops of soda cans — from home or the side of the road or wherever they could find them — and she had helpers come to her homeroom and count them. Her goal was to get to one million. That's what she said in the article. She said she wanted students to see what a million looked like.

It took her students eight years to collect a million pull tabs. When she got to one million, she threw a party for all the students who'd helped her count over the years, and then recycled the metal and donated the recycling money to an environmental group that was taking care of the Schuylkill River. She was quoted in the article saying trash was collective — it was all of ours. She said, "If we don't start paying attention to our trash, it will pile up."

I didn't know if anyone learned from the experiment other than the kids who helped her. People still tossed trash anywhere they wanted because I still saw trash on the side of the road all the time. And in parking lots. And in the creek.

This year was Ms. G's last year as a teacher. I was so glad I got to have her. Every April she celebrated Earth Month because she felt that Earth Day wasn't enough. She was a legend not only in the school and the community, but in my house, because Bernadette had her the same year as Mr. Mustache bullied her, and Ms. G saved her by being nice, because Ms. G is always nice.

"Your generation ruined the planet," Bernadette said to Dad as she landed on St. James Place.

"I didn't personally ruin the planet," Dad said. "I don't know who told you I did, but whoever it is, is lying. And you owe me two hundred dollars." He smiled and held his hand out to Bernadette.

"Plastics," I said. "Plastics ruined everything."

Once Bernadette paid Dad his two hundred dollars, he said, "*Plastics ruined everything?* Tell me how plastics ruined everything." He walked to the fridge and opened the door. He pointed at each thing as he named it. "The milk comes in plastic, the cheese, the eggs, the apple juice. All the meat is wrapped in plastic. The butter, the yogurt, sour cream, fruit cups for your lunch, carrots, tomatoes, and lettuce — all in plastic." He looked in the shelves in the fridge door (which were made of plastic). "Chocolate syrup! Strawberry syrup! Mayonnaise! Ketchup! Barbecue sauce, mustard, lemon juice!"

Bernadette looked at me and I looked at her and I didn't know what she was thinking, but I was thinking that maybe we should shut up now before I lost outside privileges for the rest of the week. I rolled and didn't roll doubles again, so I stayed in jail.

I said, "You're right, Dad. What I said was stupid."

"You bet it was stupid. Look around this kitchen. Look around this house. Plastic. And it isn't ruining anything."

"It's been proven to cause cancer in rats," Bernadette said.

Dad answered, "At this point, I think everything causes cancer in rats. How do you know rats aren't just susceptible to cancer?"

Bernadette sighed. Dad rolled the dice. He landed on the one property where Bernadette had a hotel and he owed her a thousand and fifty dollars.

We didn't talk about anything else but the game until it was over. Dad won. Of course.

I cleaned up while Bernadette checked her phone for text messages. Dad went upstairs to change out of his work clothes. When

33

I put the Monopoly box back in the cabinet in the den, I heard the cry of the animal I'd left at the creek. It sounded like it was in the driveway. It was part howl and part screech, like a baby who missed its mother.

I opened the back door and stood on the porch. I heard the animal running toward me, but I couldn't see anything until the sensor light went on and the animal stopped in the bright light. It had my flashlight in its mouth, clamped in its under-biting jaw. I heard a sound by the window and saw Bernadette looking out at me.

The animal dropped my flashlight and ran back toward the creek.

By the time Bernadette came outside I was testing my flashlight and it worked. I acted like nothing big had happened, but on the inside, I was feeling better than I had in more than six months. I wanted to find the animal and make it my friend because bringing my flashlight back was the nicest thing anyone had ever done for me, outside of Annie Bell carrying extra tissues in case I got a nosebleed on the bus.

"What was that?" Bernadette asked.

"What was what?"

"That noise."

"I don't know," I said. "I didn't hear anything."

CHAPTER 8

PLASTIC TREATS & PUTRID ANNIE

There was wailing. There had always been wailing. Before the field was flattened, it was a mourning dove and a screech owl and a fox sometimes. Now it was an animal I didn't understand.

My alarm on school days usually didn't go off until 6:25 but I couldn't sleep past 5:30 on Tuesday morning because the animal wailed all night. I got up and walked out toward the creek with two plastic shopping bags and an empty milk jug in my hand. The minute the animal saw me, it started running toward me like it was my pet. I ran toward it too, because I didn't want Mom or Dad to see us out their bedroom window.

When we met halfway to the creek, it nudged its head into me and then backed away and wagged its nubby tail and followed me. I kept walking to the creek. The animal made grunting noises and galloped — or just loped. It walked like a dog but grunted like a pig. And it was a he. I won't tell you how I knew, but I knew. It was a he.

I said, "Thanks for finding my flashlight."

He grunted.

I said, "I really appreciate it."

The animal grunted again and stared at the plastic milk jug in my hand. I gave him the jug and he settled on the bank and started munching. He had a grin on his face and his tail-nub kept wagging. He seemed to like hard plastic more than the bags.

This was the first time I'd seen him in decent light. He seemed confused—all his parts were mixed up. His back end was dog, except for the nubby tail. His front end was porcine, which was a fancy name for pig-like. His hooves were weird because he had toes. His face was pointy on top, but he had an under bite like a hog. His nose was like someone stuck a dog's nose on the end of a tapir's snout. He didn't have whiskers. Not even little ones. His hair was probably under all that slimy algae. Or maybe he was just made of slime. I couldn't tell. Either way, I wanted us to be friends.

The first step of being friends: Stop calling your new friend *the animal*.

"What's your name?" I asked.

He just thumped his tail and kept munching.

I ran through all the normal names in my head. Normal boy names. *Bobby, Billy, Johnny, Matt, Tyler, Chris*. Normal pet names. *Spot, Dexter, Buddy, Killer*. None of them fit. The animal walked over to me and nudged me and I pulled out a plastic shopping bag from my pocket. Before I could get it all the way out, he snapped it between his teeth and sucked it into his mouth. I made sure he didn't get all the shopping bags in one mouthful.

I wanted to sit and watch the sun rise with him. The sun always rose in the east and east was over behind *Phase One* and *Phase Two* now, so we'd have to watch it rise over the roofs of *New Spacious Homes!* The light was coming from behind the development and it looked like fire.

I thought about what Dad said the night before about how everything we use comes in plastic packaging. I thought about the plastic siding on the new houses. Mostly beige plastic. Tan. Ash. All dull colors. I thought about Monopoly and I looked out to *Phase One* and *Phase Two* and I pictured Dad holding out his hand every time I landed on Marvin Gardens, where he'd built his big red plastic hotel.

"Marvin," I said.

The animal kept sucking on the plastic bag.

"Your name is Marvin," I said again. "Marvin Gardens."

He didn't care what his name was. He nudged my side again and I gave him another plastic shopping bag to eat.

"Do you like it? I think it fits."

I checked my watch and knew I had to go back home and pretend I'd just woken up.

I threw him the milk jug cap and said, "See you after school."

He was so excited by the hard plastic treat that he stopped sucking on the bag and chewed up the cap. The noise was still loud, but it wasn't scary anymore.

I wished I could sit there with him all day.

At breakfast a half hour later, nobody seemed to notice I'd been gone. As I ate my Cheerios, I tried to figure out if I should say I was sick and stay home. But I couldn't stay home without a fever.

When I got to the bus stop, everyone was already there. I timed it like that so I didn't have to wait long. Tommy and his new friends always sat on the curb and talked about things like Pokémon, comic books, and girls. I stood on the sidewalk and looked toward the creek, my back to them.

These were the slowest minutes of my day. Bus minutes.

Tommy's new friends were complaining about how they had two tests in one day.

"I bet Obe studied," Tommy said.

I could feel them all looking at me but I didn't turn around.

"He's such a good boy!" Tommy said, the way you say it to a dog when the dog did something right. "Such a good, good boy!" His friends laughed. I kept my back to them. The other kids at the bus stop just stood there, waiting. None of them knew that I'd just discovered a brand-new species of animal.

The bus rounded the corner from Gilbrand Road and we all got on it. Tommy and his friends went first and walked toward the back. I sat in seat twelve because it was my seat.

We had seating assignments on the bus. Six months ago Tommy switched to sit with his new friend Mike, and the bus driver told him that it was the only switch he'd get. In the switch, I got to sit next to Annie Bell, who the boys called Putrid Annie because she threw up in school once. Annie was in the fifth grade and moved here from Portland, Oregon, right before winter break. She lived in *Phase One*. I liked her because she was the one kid on the bus who wasn't trying to prove something to anyone. She said the boys who called her Putrid Annie were just dumb and weak because they couldn't think for themselves.

That was probably true. The only thing I really knew about Mike, Tommy's new best friend, was that he'd accidentally shot his younger brother in the foot with a BB gun when he was little. His brother still had the BB in his foot. I'd seen it. Other than that, Mike didn't seem to have much of a personality. He didn't have hobbies. He didn't get good grades. He didn't care about much.

Annie cared about pretty much everything. She loved two things especially: rocks and weather. She wanted to be a geologist or a meteorologist. Whenever she found a rock, she'd talk about how old it might be, and she told me all about the geologic time scale, which was like pretending the Earth was a cake, with layers, and some layers were older than other layers. She also believed the weather in Portland, Oregon, was superior to the weather in Reading, Pennsylvania, so we'd argue about that sometimes — but never really argue-argue. I wished, for Annie, that Ms. G wasn't retiring this year. Of all the science-loving people in the world, Annie deserved Ms. G.

Annie played the cello, so on orchestra days, she'd have to fit both herself and her cello into our seat. Because of how big the cello was, she had to squeeze in close to me and put the cello in the aisle seat. I didn't mind. There was nothing putrid about Annie.

"What's wrong with you?" she asked when she got on that morning.

"What?"

"You look happy or something."

"I can't be happy?"

"Not on a Tuesday, no," she said. "You're supposed to be mopey and kind of annoyed."

I laughed.

"Oh my gosh. You're laughing now? That's worrying."

"Stop it or I'll laugh more," I said.

"I'll be you, then. Look. Mopey. Annoyed." She held her face in this frozen look of pain.

Is that what it was like to be my friend? To have to look at that all the time? The bus was worse than anywhere else, I knew that. Tommy and his new friends were there. Maybe I was happier off the bus, but I couldn't tell. It's hard to see yourself when you're yourself, I guess.

Annie still had that look on her face — like she was trying hard to look mean or something.

"You can stop now," I said.

"Good." She smiled. "It's tiring being you."

I reached into my pocket and found the tiny rock I'd picked up at the creek. I gave it to her.

"Oooo! Quartzite!" she said. "Good job, rock hound."

I smiled.

That day was the slowest school day I ever experienced. Tuesday's Earth Month fact: *Fourteen billion pounds of garbage is dumped into the ocean every year and most of it is plastic. Remember to recycle when you can!* I was glad Ms. G put those announcements on every day in April, but sometimes they were depressing. I collected trash from my creek every day. Who was collecting fourteen billion pounds of garbage from the ocean every year? It was enough to make me cry, so I stopped thinking about it.

All I could really think about the whole day was Marvin — what he was, where he came from, what he looked like. I didn't get any nosebleeds, which was nice, and Ms. G started a new environment unit about the different types of pollution. In the beginning of class, she reminded us that we should start thinking about our final project for Earth Month because it counted as a big part of our grade. The final project was a contest — like a science fair but just in our classroom. Luckily she handed out a sheet with all the information on it because I just sat there and daydreamed about bringing Marvin in as my project. He ate plastic. He might be an undiscovered species. How could I not win with that?

Annie and I talked about Portland, Oregon, on the bus because she missed home.

"Have you ever seen the Pacific Ocean?" she asked me.

"No."

"It's better than the Atlantic," she said.

"How do you know? I mean, aren't they both just oceans?"

"The Pacific is bigger, for one thing."

"Well, that doesn't prove anything," I said. "Anyway, it's colder, isn't it? You can't swim in it."

"That's wrong. You can totally swim in it."

"Isn't there a giant island of trash in the Pacific Ocean?" I asked. I'd heard about it on TV. Even Dad talked about it.

"That's stupid," Annie said.

"I'm serious. There's, like, an island the size of Texas made out of trash."

"Either way, it's better than the Atlantic Ocean."

Just to mess with her, I said, "I'm partial to the Arctic."

"Well, you definitely can't swim in *that*!"

And then Annie's stop came and she got off the bus and I had to wait three more stops to get to our bus stop.

I walked slowly around the new road and looked toward the creek but I couldn't see Marvin. I knew my mom was home so I couldn't just go down there or she'd get worried. So I went home for a snack and to see if there was any more stuff in the recycling bin.

But then Mom was waiting at the kitchen table with that look on her face like I was in trouble. It turned out my jerkface mustached math teacher had written her a letter about how I hadn't been doing my homework. I was almost failing his class. I'd never failed anything in my whole life.

CHAPTER 9

QUESTIONS & MEAT LOAF

There were questions. There were always questions.

"Are you even following along in class?" Mom asked.

"Kind of," I said. "The homework is just boring. Work sheets all the time."

"Even if you don't like work sheets, you still have to do them," she said. "It's homework."

"He said he'd let me do them again," I said. "He gave me a packet."

"He says you failed the test too. That means you lied to us yesterday."

I didn't say anything.

She said, "If you fall behind in math now, in sixth grade, it will get harder year after year. You'll miss important things."

I wanted to tell her about why Mr. Mustache hated me, but I didn't because it would get Bernadette in trouble for what she'd done to him when she was in sixth grade.

Mom pointed upstairs. "Go to your room and do the work sheets."

I sighed. "Can I at least go to the creek first?"

"No."

"After dinner?"

"No."

"But what if I have them all done by then?"

"No." She didn't even look at me.

When I got to my room, I cried. I punched the pillows on my bed. I even cursed a few times under my breath. The whole idea of punishing me this way was dumb because I didn't want to do the stupid work sheets *before* I got punished. Now I didn't want to do them at all.

Mr. Mustache was boring. All work sheets and discipline. Three years ago he caught Bernadette writing in her journal during math class and he didn't just confiscate it. He read it. Bernadette had been reading books about spies and she kept good notes on Mr. Mustache. Mr. Mustache didn't appreciate what she wrote and he held a grudge. The first thing he said to me when I walked into his classroom in sixth grade was, "So you're the other Devlin kid, huh? Hope you're smarter than your sister." If I was a dog, I'd have growled at him and clamped on to his leg for talking bad about Bernadette. But I was Obe Devlin. I just sat there and glared at him, and now I tried my best not to fall asleep in his boring stupid work sheet class.

I picked up a notebook and tried to draw Marvin Gardens. I wasn't very good at drawing, so I kept trying until the dinner bell.

Dinner was meat loaf.

Dinner was more questions.

Dad said, "I don't understand. Why would you lie to us?"

"I don't know."

"It's just math. You like math," he said.

I just nodded and ate my meat loaf.

"You're getting too wrapped up in what's going on around here," Mom said. "The field and the developments and noise. It's probably my fault. I made too big of a deal out of all of it."

"No, you didn't," I said. "It's bad. It's worse for you anyway because you lived here all your life."

"You didn't make too big of a deal out of it, Mom," Bernadette said. "We're all sad."

"I'm not sad," Dad said.

"You're addicted to Monopoly," Bernadette said.

"I'm not *addicted*."

"You make us play twice a week at least. And it's *Monopoly*, Dad. Can't you see the connection?" she answered.

"Men just deal with things different to women," he said. "Isn't that right, Obe? We fix things. We don't cry. We solve problems."

"There's no solution to this problem," I said.

"It's almost over now anyway," Mom said. "We should just get on with our lives and get used to the new neighborhood."

"And you need to stop wasting your time out at that creek," Dad said to me. "Obviously it's now interfering with your homework."

"It wasn't the creek," I said.

When I said this, I got a nosebleed. Right then, as if the universe wanted my parents to know that something was wrong but I couldn't tell them. As I got a few tissues and folded them up and put them to my nose, I excused myself to the couch to get horizontal.

I took out my favorite book from our small bookshelf next to the couch — *The Atlas of World History*. It was cooler than any social studies book at school because it was arranged by dates and had timelines and maps. Maps helped me learn and remember stuff better. I flipped around the pages and read interesting facts from a thousand years ago and fifty years ago. I replaced the tissues on my nose every ten minutes or so. The nosebleed was slowing down by the time Bernadette did the dishes. Dad walked by me to go to the bathroom in the den, but he didn't even ask me how I was doing. I kept my head buried in the book and was glad they didn't ask questions. If they did, I might have to tell them why I had the nosebleeds, and Dad wouldn't be happy about that story at all.

CHAPTER 10

PHEASANTS & ORCHARDS

There were turf wars, over and over again on these acres. One hundred years ago, it was a war between my great-grandfather and the bank's mortgage officer. More than two hundred years before that, the Lenape tribe had their land traded out from under them by King Charles II, who didn't even own it.

Six months ago, my best friend Tommy punched me in the nose. Except he wasn't my best friend anymore. And technically he sucker punched me.

It wasn't a fair fight.

Since kindergarten, we had been the only two kids at our bus stop. Our stop was just a place on the side of Gilbrand Road with some gravel and a little bit of extra road shoulder so we wouldn't get hit by drivers on their way to or from work. It was halfway between his house and my house.

Now there were so many houses I couldn't count them all. During *Phase One,* they erected a huge sign with a map of numbered building lots and the name of the development, THE ORCHARDS. Of course they had to tear down the actual orchards to build the houses. Up Gilbrand Road a half mile there was a new development called PHEASANT'S NEST. No more pheasants nested there. *Phase Two* was called OAK TRAIL but they had to cut down the two-hundred-year-old oak tree to . . . You get the picture.

Bernadette taught me about the word *irony* using these development names. Irony was when something was deliberately opposite of what it meant to be and was therefore funny. But in this case, it wasn't so funny for the oak tree or the pheasants or the orchard. Or me.

By fourth grade, there were thirteen more kids at our bus stop. Thirteen. They had to move our bus stop to Orchard Way because it wasn't safe to have fifteen kids standing on the gravel shoulder. Tommy and I made a pact that we wouldn't be friends with anyone who lived in any of these ironically named places. That pact lasted a whole year. We weren't mean or anything. We didn't not talk to them at the bus stop. We just didn't join in their games or conversations. They seemed fine with that because they were suburban kids and we were country kids. One kid named Mike used to make fun of Tommy's sneakers because they weren't brand name, and I told him that he should stop because country kids knew how to fight. That shut him up.

Of course we didn't know how to fight. We just knew a lot about nature and tadpoles and the farm equipment the farmer used to bring at harvest time, and we knew about slurry. Suburban kids didn't really know about slurry. The kids from *Phase One* always held their noses as if fertilizing the soil was less important than the air smelling good. That was back when there were still crops and a farmer and farm equipment in *Phase Three*.

Anyway, by October of fifth grade, Tommy ended up with a pair of brand-name sneakers. And then after school, he brought Mike with him to the creek. Mike—the kid who'd made fun of his sneakers. Tommy even started acting suburban. He put gel in his hair and everything.

One hundred years ago, I bet this same stuff happened too. I bet best friends got new friends and bought the right kind of shoes to fit in with the kids at school.

By summer Mike brought John and John brought Dylan and there were too many boys at my creek. I tried to be friends with them, but they only talked about video games and they rolled their eyes whenever I found an interesting animal track. One day in August, right before my eleventh birthday, Dylan had a pocket full of candy and he shared it with us and we were all sitting on the log bridge. As each boy ate his candy, he dropped the wrapper into the creek. First John, then Dylan, then Mike. I looked at Tommy and he knew I was upset, and a real best friend would say, "Hey guys! Don't drop your trash into Obe's creek!" But he didn't say that. Instead, he dropped his candy wrapper in too.

I said, "Hey! Stop littering in my creek!"

Mike said, "Don't be stupid."

John said, "Who cares?"

Dylan said, "That's the last time I'm bringing you candy!"

Tommy jumped down into the creek and got his wrapper and put it in his pocket. I dropped down and got the others' wrappers and put them in my pocket. The other boys called us hippies.

And even though Tommy did that, I knew he wasn't going to be my best friend after that day. At the last summer league baseball game the next week, Mike told me that Tommy told him that I was a hippie and he didn't really like me anymore.

I knew better than to believe interlopers, so I asked Tommy myself and he said, "You're still such a little kid. We're eleven now!"

"So being eleven means I can't care about kids throwing trash in my creek?"

"It's not your creek," he said.

"It's called Devlin Creek. It's on my land."

"Yeah, but it's all of ours. Not just yours."

This was the beginning.

CHAPTER 11

ONE HUNDRED YEARS AGO

One hundred years ago, mean people formed mobs. One hundred years ago, a man named Jesse Washington was murdered by a mob in Texas. One hundred years ago, white people all over this country thought they were better than black people like Jesse Washington. Hasn't changed in some minds. I heard all kinds of stupid stuff on the bus when kids moved into the new neighborhood. Luis moved here from Cuba a year ago and none of Tommy's boys ever talked to him. Said he couldn't speak English. Said his accent was stupid. I liked Luis. And his accent.

One hundred years ago, my great-grandfather got into a bar fight because someone said something bad about the Irish. People used to make fun of the Irish the way they made fun of people like Luis now. My great-grandfather broke a man's arm by throwing him right across the barroom after the man said that the Irish were all stupid drunks and should go back to dumb, rainy Ireland. My great-grandfather was only a quarter Irish—he was more English and German than anything—but it didn't matter. The police came to the farm the next day. In the end, my great-grandfather didn't have to go to jail, but he owed a fine of $500. Twenty more acres mortgaged.

CHAPTER 12

EARLY BIRDS & BLUE FOOD

There were early birds. They were getting worms, I guessed.

I'd set my alarm for five thirty. I hadn't heard Marvin crying like the night before. There was nothing left in our recycling bin so I grabbed a handful of plastic bags and an empty yogurt container that was sitting in the sink.

I had a whole hour before I had to go back inside and pretend to wake up. I tiptoed to the creek, careful not to be seen by anyone. The place was empty. It was quiet this early — except for the early birds.

I saw Marvin through the tree line over in *Phase Three*, wandering in the space-like landscape. He put his snout in the air and then turned his head right for me and ran. He made me laugh. Marvin was hilarious when he ran. Goofy. It made me think of Annie and how she'd made me laugh the day before. That's what friends do. They make you laugh, I guess. He splashed through the creek and hopped up onto the bank next to me. When he saw me laughing, he smiled. I looked around again in case anyone would see us. It felt like we were on the moon. I scratched his head and gave him a plastic bag and the yogurt container. "Sorry, buddy. It's all we have."

He crunched on the yogurt container and took the bag from me and sat down next to it.

"So where did you come from?" I asked. "I mean, I can't tell if you evolved or if you're from somewhere else or what." I thought about Marvin maybe being from space. I stopped thinking about that as soon as I started. I'd take Bigfoot over an alien any day. "Wherever you came from, I'm glad you came. It was kind of lonely out here until you showed up."

He sucked the bag into his mouth and started munching on it.

"So, what's your deal? Do you only eat plastic or do you eat other stuff?" I asked. "You have to eat something nutritious, right? Those bags can't be nutritious."

Marvin kept noshing on the bag, and I realized that this was going to be a very one-sided friendship when it came to talking.

"Did you know that development used to have a big oak tree in it?" I pointed to *Phase Two*, now called OAK TRAIL. "I always wanted to climb it. Mom said she used to climb it when she was little. She said it was probably close to two hundred years old when they cut it down. I was too little to climb it then."

Marvin looked interested, so I kept talking. "That over there used to be Mr. Willard's orchard." I pointed to *Phase One,* THE

ORCHARDS. "We used to go apple picking, and Mom says Mr. Willard used to pay her four bucks an hour when she was a kid to pick up windfalls. A windfall is an apple that falls off the tree in the wind. Mr. Willard used to sell those at half price. Mom used to make applesauce out of them."

Marvin seemed unimpressed.

"This whole place used to be my family's farm," I said. "But now we just have this part. We own the woods over there too, but I'm not allowed to go over there anymore because . . ."

I could never finish this sentence.

"Wanna go see some houses?"

I walked across the bridge while he sloshed back through the creek. I crossed through the tree line and arrived in *Phase Three*. *Phase Three* didn't have a name yet. If they asked me, I could give them one. There were plenty of things that were here once and are gone now. CORNFIELD HAVEN, FLYING GEESE MEADOWS, BUCK RUN, COYOTE CROSSING.

We stayed out of sight—not too close to the road and not too close to any finished houses. Marvin grunted along next to me and found little snacks along the way. A plastic bottle cap—his favorite, it seemed, which made that horrible sound when he chewed it—and a piece of plastic binding from construction materials. He could eat and walk at the same time. He heeled by my side just like a dog.

We walked down the new road and there were two newly built basements—cement blocks and floors and that's all. On the other side of the road there were two houses that were half-built.

The frames were up, the roofs were on, the windows and doors still had those stickers all over them, and the front porches were in place, cement covered in mud. I stepped up onto the porch and Marvin stopped where the ground stopped. I said, "Come on! It's okay!" but he stayed out of the house. I walked through the first floor and saw the plywood subflooring and the insulation between the joists, and if I closed my eyes, I could see the whole house coming together.

During *Phase One*, I had thought I might want to be an architect because when you walk around enough unfinished houses, you get a feel for how they're designed. But then I realized if I did that, I'd be taking away some kid's cornfield.

Now I didn't know what I wanted to be. A scientist, maybe. A veterinarian, maybe. (Bernadette always said stuff like, "Animals are Obe's *groove!*") Something where I could help nature and be cool and nerdy at the same time. Something Ms. G would approve of. Something where I could be Creek Boy forever. Annie and I talked about being professors sometimes. She said, "I want to have the word *doctor* in front of my name. Dr. Annie Bell. What do you think?" I told her she would make a great professor. She said I'd make a good professor too, but I couldn't see myself being called Dr. Obe Devlin. It didn't seem to fit me as much as it fit her.

When I came out to the porch again, I found Marvin gnawing on a piece of plumbing tubing. It was blue. I was known to eat everything, any time, except blue food. (This didn't include blueberries because technically, they were purple.) I said, "Buddy, you should never trust blue food."

As Marvin and I walked back toward the wild patch, I squatted down and picked up a few rocks for Annie. Marvin squatted down to poop. I looked away because it's weird to watch something poop. With my back turned, I heard him making grunty poop noises and I laughed a little because sometimes I made poop noises and Mom told me I was too old for that. It must be cool to be an animal and not ever have to stop making grunty poop noises.

Then a smell wafted its way over to where I was standing. It was disgusting. It was worse than pig slurry times a hundred. Nothing — *NOTHING* — in the history of the world ever smelled worse than the smell of Marvin's poop.

I left him there by himself and walked to the creek. My eyes were watering. I pulled my sweatshirt up over my nose, but even when I was all the way at the creek, I could smell it. It was the kind of stink that would stay in my nostrils for the rest of the day.

When Marvin finished his business, he came to the creek, but I was still so overwhelmed by the smell I just started walking to escape it. We ended up on the suburban sidewalk that linked *Phase Two* and *Phase Three*. A few people were up already. Old people and runners. Runners are always up early. At the end of Oak Trail Way, which was the original path to the oak tree, there was a man who had his garage door open. He looked like he was just about to start his lawn mower and cut his grass. At six o'clock on a Wednesday morning.

I kept walking to escape the smell. I didn't think I'd ever get rid of it. I wasn't sure what to think of Marvin just then. I still liked him. He was still my friend. But I'd have to avoid ever having to deal with his poop again. Talk about nasty.

Then the old guy about to get on his lawn mower looked at us sideways. And then I remembered Marvin, now loping a yard behind me, and how he wasn't a dog or a cat or a raccoon or a skunk or anything anyone had ever seen before.

When I said "Run!" Marvin knew what to do. He ran.

CHAPTER 13

NOXIOUS SCAT & THE SNITCH

There were germs.

A lot of kids were missing from the bus stop—I'd heard a spring cold was going around. I stood there and wondered if anyone else could smell Marvin's noxious scat. That's what they called poop in my animal track guide. *Scat.* I couldn't stop smelling it, even after going home and washing my face and brushing my teeth and eating two bowls of Cheerios.

Three stops after I got on, Annie climbed up the steps with her cello, and for the rest of the ride, Tommy and his friends said stuff to us. "Bet that big violin has more interesting things to say than the hippie!" I thought I heard Tommy laughing. It still hurt me, if I had to be honest, that my best and only friend for so long could be this dumb because a bunch of other boys moved in. But then

I looked back and Tommy wasn't laughing at all. He was just sitting there.

I wanted to talk to Annie and make her laugh but I didn't have anything to say because all I wanted to do was tell her about Marvin. They were my only friends. They should know each other. And yet, I wanted to keep Marvin to myself. I know this sounds selfish, but when everything that was yours is gone, and then everything that's left gets ruined by a kid who used to be your best friend, you just want to hold on to things or something. Annie deserved better from me. I knew that. But after all that destruction—he came to see me on my turf. Marvin was mine. He was meant to be mine.

I pulled out the rocks I'd picked up for her.

"Dude!" She held up a rock. "This thing is probably five hundred million years old."

"That old?"

"Around here, yeah. Could be a little younger. Four hundred million. You can't tell by just looking at them. It's limestone. Pretty common."

I wondered how old Marvin was. I knew he wasn't common, anyway.

•••

Wednesday's Earth Month announcement fact was: *Pollution kills a million seabirds every year.* I'd been hearing these facts every April since I was in first grade but since meeting Marvin, they were making me sadder than they used to.

There was another Mr. Mustache math quiz. I knew it was coming and I still didn't do my makeup work sheets and I didn't study. I guessed the answers but I didn't even know what we were working on. I just kept thinking about Marvin. How he ate plastic. How bad his scat smelled. I knew there had to be a connection between the two—the same way that when I ate ice cream, I got diarrhea. Maybe Marvin was sick. Maybe he wasn't supposed to be eating plastic. Maybe he was crazy or something.

In science class, Ms. G showed us pictures of dead baby albatrosses. You could see their skeletons because they had decomposed and were just lying there with everything exposed. The worst part of the pictures, one after the other, were the contents of the baby albatrosses' stomachs. They were filled with brightly colored tiny plastic items. Little red plastic beads. Little squares of orange plastic from whatever made little squares of orange plastic. The nature in the pictures was the right color—the bones and the feathers and the beak and the rock where the albatrosses lay, but there, centered, were the reds, oranges, blues, greens. Unnatural. Not meant to be eaten. Killers.

I felt like I'd been punched in the nose all over again.

Then Ms. G showed us a few more pictures—pictures of water samples collected from the Great Pacific Garbage Patch. It wasn't an island like a big floating blob of plastic bottles we could climb on. It was more like a huge area of the ocean where the water was so intensely polluted that a glassful looked like thousands of pieces of plastic confetti suspended in a sort of gel. This was not the ocean. That's what I kept telling myself as she showed us more and more pictures. This. Was. Not. The. Ocean.

But it was the ocean. It *is* the ocean.

For the rest of the day, I walked around school suspended in that gel. A piece of confetti poised to be swallowed by a baby albatross. Ready to wash back out to sea to kill more baby albatrosses. I felt as small as that. What could an eleven-year-old kid from Gilbrand Road do about a problem so big? Bigger than *New Spacious Homes!* Bigger than twenty cement trucks. Bigger than 175 acres of lost land. Bigger than anything I could ever imagine.

By the time we were on the bus home, Annie, her cello, and I sat quietly in seat twelve and the bus driver had to yell at some of the new kids to quiet down and to stay sitting while the bus was moving. Mike was showing off the BB in his little brother's foot. All the kids wanted to get a look at it. When I turned around to look, Tommy was sitting in the same seat as Mike, but he was pressed up against the window, looking out. There was no way Tommy was having as good a time with him as he'd had with me.

I didn't say a word to Annie. I smiled and acted nice, so it wasn't like I was mean. But I was still suspended in gel, so I just said "See you tomorrow" when she got to her stop and stood up to leave. As the bus approached my bus stop, I thought I saw Mom standing there, which she never did. *It couldn't be Mom. She never meets me off the bus. I'm too old for that.*

But it was her, and I was embarrassed and then concerned. When Tommy's grandfather died, his mom met him at the bus stop out on Gilbrand Road. We started walking away from the other kids that got off the bus and Mom didn't say anything.

"Did someone die?" I asked. Dad's parents lived in Florida. Mom only had her mom left, who lived in Arizona.

"We'll talk about it at home," she said.

"You have to tell me if somebody died now because it's not fair to wait until we're home."

"Nobody died."

"Okay," I said. "Good."

When we got home, this is what we talked about: The old neighbor lawn mower guy told her I was out walking at six o'clock in the morning.

What a snitch. That's what I said. "What a snitch."

"He was worried," she said.

"About what?"

"You could get hit by a car or something. We wouldn't even know you were out there," she said. "You could go, you know, missing."

"That guy watches too much TV," I said. *Missing.* Seriously.

Mom took a gulp of her tea and said, "He said you were walk-ing a dog. Is that true?"

"No."

"Weird. He said he saw a dog."

"We don't have a dog," I said.

She looked at me like she was thinking, *Duh, Obe, I know we don't have a dog.*

"I just woke up early and wanted to go see the creek," I said.

63

"You're grounded."

"What? For what? I didn't do anything!"

"Your father and I talked about it and we agreed that if you can't stay safe outside, then we'd have to keep you in for a few days. Plus, you need to catch up on your homework. I checked your grades on the computer today, and your math teacher left another note for me."

"I'm doing my work!" I said. This was a complete lie.

"What was today's quiz about?" she asked.

I sat there and tried so hard to remember the quiz. I tried to remember the heading on today's work sheet. I froze just like when I thought Marvin Gardens was eating my liver.

I was grounded. For three days.

Dad caught me crying about it later that night. He said, "Toughen up. Boys don't cry about stuff like this."

I didn't know what *stuff like this* meant. I don't really know why I was crying. It wasn't just because I was grounded. I had more than one reason to cry.

"You messed up and you got caught," Dad said. "So what? When I was a kid blah blah blah and blah blah blah and it taught me a lesson. Just do the work. Be brave!" That was Dad's line. He told me more than once that boys should be fearless, daring, and brave. I was being more fearless, daring, and brave than ever since Marvin Gardens showed up, but since I couldn't tell anyone about Marvin, no one could know how brave I really was.

Three days felt like a week. My mosquito bites started healing. Even though the windows were open, I felt like I needed fresh air.

Every dinner tasted bland. Every conversation was boring. Even Bernadette seemed to be disappointed in me. She said, "Dude, just sit down and do the stupid work sheets. Stop being so stubborn."

But all I did until the weekend was draw pictures of Marvin Gardens. I wondered if there were more of him. He couldn't be the only one, could he? Maybe they all ate plastic by the ton. Maybe they could be the solution. The pollution solution. That's what I thought when I drew the pictures. *Marvin Gardens — the pollution solution.*

I hid the notebook every morning where no one would find it. I rode the bus. I talked to Annie Bell about El Niño, her newest weather fascination. I cried in my room where my dad couldn't see me. I didn't do my makeup Mr.-Mustache-stupid-work-sheet homework. I overheard Mom say to Dad on Thursday night that I was "prematurely becoming a rebellious teenager."

That couldn't have been further from the truth. I wanted to go back in time, not forward. I wanted to go back to first grade and figure out how to make the whole thing never happen. No *Phase Anything.* No tree mulchers. No dirt diggers. No house seeds. No ironic development names. Even if it meant I would never meet Marvin Gardens, that would have been fine with me.

CHAPTER 14

ONE HUNDRED YEARS AGO

One hundred years ago, my great-grandfather's tomato crop wasn't doing so well. The year before, his oat crop succumbed to a virus. My great-grandfather thought his crop had plant lice — aphids — and he was right, but what he didn't know is that the aphids were spreading a virus called barley yellow dwarf, which they didn't even know about one hundred years ago. The harvest was barely there. When he planted the tomatoes in 1916, it was an attempt to grow a high-priced crop to make up for the past year's failure. When he saw the tomato leaves starting to curl, he went to Hannah's Bar and talked to his friends. They said not to worry. They said it was dry and a bit of rain would help.

One hundred years ago, a newlywed couple dropped into Hannah's Bar for a drink. Most of the men in the bar paid no notice, but my great-grandfather watched them and thought of his wife, and he regretted treating her poorly for so long. He bought a ring with a pearl set in it and gave it to her when he got home that night. My great-grandmother was not happy about this. She asked him how much it cost and when she asked, he gave her a bloody nose. That's how things were in my family one hundred years ago. It may be sad, but it's the truth.

CHAPTER 15

BELLY RUBS & *PROBLEMS*

There was a tennis ball. I picked it up from the dirt and realized it was probably Tommy's, but it was on my turf, so it was mine. It was Saturday morning and I was free. I threw it for Marvin and he fetched it. I told him to stay, holding my hand out. He stayed. He knew what to do when I said, "Down!" He sat.

Marvin tried to eat the tennis ball and I said, "No!" and he stopped. He was smarter than your average wild animal, that's for sure. I practiced the commands with him a few more times while tossing the tennis ball for him to fetch, and just when I thought we were getting somewhere with his training, he dropped the ball and loped to the creek, stepped into the current, and floated along with it downstream.

Marvin didn't come back to the creek all day. I got so bored I did a few sheets of makeup math homework.

Bernadette and I made our own dinner. Easy freezer-to-oven food. We ate early because we were hungry. Mom would be home from work at seven. Dad, not until after the mall closed.

Marvin Gardens showed up after dinner. When I said I was going outside, Bernadette said I had to be back soon. Saturdays were movie nights and Bernadette wanted to watch something scary. I looked for my trowel and something to bury. In my room were ten Matchbox cars. I never played with the cars, so I wouldn't miss them. I stopped on the back porch to grab the few plastic things that were in our recycling bin.

Imagine that. I used to bring home plastic *from* the creek, and now I took plastic *to* the creek.

As Marvin sat next to me on the bank and thumped his tail and ate two plastic yogurt containers, I talked to him about stupid stuff, mostly.

"Do you think boys should have feelings?" I said. "Because I think it's stupid that my dad thinks boys shouldn't have feelings. I mean, I have them already. I'm not sure how to get rid of them."

Marvin kept eating.

"You know, I never even liked baseball. I like watching Bernadette play softball because she's really good and she likes playing it and you can tell she's happy when she's doing it. I only played baseball because Dad said I was supposed to. But I'd rather just hang out here with you and talk and stuff," I said.

If I looked at him the right way, he was kind of smiling at me. I smiled too and that made him roll over onto his back. He made a noise like he was laughing.

I can't lie — it was hard to rub his slimy belly. If he were fluff-ier or less smelly, it would have been easier to be physically close to him, but between the slime, the weird noises that he made, and the nasty waste he produced, Marvin was a pretty gross pet. Or friend. Or whatever he was.

I rubbed his belly anyway and it wasn't that bad once I got used to it.

He wanted to roughhouse like a dog then. I wrestled with him and pushed him away. He growled and flipped around like cats do when you drive them crazy with laser lights or a toy on the end of a rope. It was cute until he nipped at my hand. He sensed my fear and didn't back down because I think animals have a different idea about playing.

Did you ever see squirrels play? They can be vicious. One time I saw three little squirrels chasing each other in a tree and one of the squirrels freaked out so much he fell all the way down to the grass. I thought he was dead but when his two friends went to check on him, chattering squirrel apologies above his motionless body, he got up and jumped right on his friend and they rolled together like nothing was wrong.

Humans can't do this.

Humans hold grudges.

Humans have *problems*.

I have wished, many times, that I was a squirrel.

•••

One hundred years ago, my great-grandfather had a *problem* — his drinking. I thought my dad had a *problem* too, only it wasn't as easy to call out. He said boys should be fearless, daring, and brave. I thought I already was, but Dad wanted me to change all the time. Clean my room. Try out for baseball. Have friends. Want to do more than pick trash out of the creek and walk around *Phase Three* remembering what it used to be like. He wanted me to be a normal boy, whatever that meant to him, not me.

The more I thought about it, the more I realized that Marvin and I had a lot in common. People probably thought animals shouldn't eat plastic. Eating plastic wasn't normal. Getting a nosebleed nearly every day wasn't normal either, but Dad never mentioned those.

•••

Marvin and I walked around for a while looking for a place to bury the cars. The workmen had been pulling out the roadside tree stumps all week — their roots all mangled and sticking out like my hair when I woke up. We walked toward the bank, passing a few of the stumps, which lay on their sides in a pile. Most of the bank where the trees used to be had been rebuilt — the earth moved to form a new bank with anti-erosion mesh on top so the rain wouldn't wash the soil away. Marvin sniffed at the anti-erosion fencing and licked it like crazy, the way a kid licks an ice cream cone. It made me wonder if there was a difference to him when it came to what he ate. Were some plastics better-tasting than others? I knew he liked the milk jug caps the way I loved ham dinners and mashed potatoes. Maybe for Marvin, anti-erosion fencing and a water bottle were as different as a cucumber and a candy bar.

"That'll be our first experiment," I said to him. "We'll find out what you like the most."

I used my trowel to bury a Matchbox car on the bank, just under the mesh, in each lot. Marvin got into the routine pretty quickly and helped me dig by putting his long nose into the hole after I dug it with the trowel. I'd drop a car in, cover it up again, stamp it down with my foot, and move to the next lot. When cars drove up and down Gilbrand Road, Marvin and I would lie flat in the dirt until they passed.

I still had three Matchbox cars left when we got to the last area of *Phase Three* where the stump holes hadn't been filled in yet and the old bank remained. Mom and Dad said building houses that close to the river was crazy because during Hurricane Agnes in 1972, the water rose so high any houses there would have been underwater all the way up to the roof.

Marvin and I walked around the lots closest to the river. He made a noise unfamiliar to me. It wasn't a bark or a howl or a snort or a whine. He was talking to someone, maybe. He was clicking and mumbling.

Between *Phase Three* and the riverbank there were railroad tracks. One hundred years ago, the train came every other day to the local grain mill and fertilizer plant. Back then people needed animal feed and fertilizer. Now, people needed whatever they made at the only factory left around here, which was about two miles up the tracks. Bernadette said it was a pantyhose factory, so I guessed people needed pantyhose. The train only came about once a week now.

The minute we stepped onto the railroad tracks, I got nervous. Eleven years of being told never (never ever ever ever ever) to go near the railroad tracks will do that to a kid. Marvin looked nervous too, so maybe he knew about railroad tracks from experience. He crossed the tracks and kept doing that talking thing with his mouth. I still had three Matchbox cars in my pocket to plant but then I heard the dinner bell.

Bernadette. Movie night.

I watched Marvin walk toward the river, still making those noises. He sounded like he was talking to his own kind. The kind of chatter you hear at normal dinner tables, probably.

The bell rang again.

I let Marvin Gardens go to wherever he was going. When I turned toward my house and started walking, he grunted a good-bye to me. I know he didn't look back because I did, and I saw him heading toward the riverbank clicking and talking louder and louder as if he already had friends down there.

On the walk home, I felt lonelier than ever.

I felt like maybe I had a *problem* too.

CHAPTER 16

GUNSHOTS & PTERODACTYLS

There was a gunshot. It woke me up.

In my family we didn't hunt. It's not that we were against hunting; it's just that my mom and dad never hunted as kids so we weren't hunters. A lot of kids around the area were hunters. In fact in my school we were allowed, as students, two days off per year to go hunting during hunting season.

But hunting season wasn't in April. Not as far as I remembered.

There was another gunshot, and I got scared for Marvin Gardens. I threw on whatever clothes were on the tops of the clothing piles in my room and ran down the hallway and the steps and out the back door. I didn't know what time it was but I knew it was early. And someone was shooting.

Only when I got outside and to the creek did I realize that the gunshots had stopped. Only when I saw Marvin Gardens wandering around out in *Phase Three* did I realize that I'd run outside in a pair of ridiculous too-short cowboy-themed pajama pants and a pink T-shirt that was Bernadette's. I guess I should have paid more attention when I was getting dressed.

Marvin saw me but didn't come over. I decided to change before I got caught wearing pajamas outside.

"Hey cowboy!" Dad said when I walked in the door.

"Oh hey."

"Up early?"

"I heard the shooting."

"So you went to the saloon to have a shootout?"

"I just—I wondered what was going on. It's the wrong time of year for hunters."

"Probably somebody shooting crows."

"Not many crows around anymore," I said.

I went to my room and put on normal clothes and then I went back downstairs.

Dad was still sitting on the den couch reading the Sunday paper. He didn't have to work on Sundays. Mom had to work every other Sunday but this was her Sunday off. That meant a Sunday roast for dinner at around two o'clock. That's how Mom grew up and that's how she was raising us. Sundays were for eating dinner at two o'clock.

"I'm going out to play," I said.

"You ready for that math test tomorrow?"

"Yep."

"Be back for Sunday dinner," he said. As I walked out the door he said, "Have you even had breakfast yet?" but I pretended not to hear him.

I stopped at the recycling bin for plastic and there was a milk jug and a sour cream container. I put them in a plastic bag, hoping to find more in the creek so I could start my experiment on Marvin and which foods he liked best.

But Marvin wasn't anywhere. Not by the creek, not in *Phase Three* (where I picked up two small pieces of plumbing tubing and a small plastic water bottle), not even down by the railroad tracks where we went the night before. I was just a kid walking around with a bag full of plastic, looking for an animal no one knew existed. Talk about *problems*.

I heard voices coming from the woods and wanted to go in and spy on the other kids. Instead, I left my bag of recycling by the creek and walked the sidewalks down through OAK TRAIL and THE ORCHARDS. I took a right up the main road and noted the ironic names of the side streets. Macintosh Way, Ambrosia Road, Pippin Lane, Jonathan Road—all varieties of apples that Mr. Willard used to grow here. I slowed down as I went by Annie's house on the corner of Orchard Way and Pippin. I heard something squeaking and I peeked into her backyard and saw her alone on her swing set. Annie had a real swing set—almost like the kind at real playgrounds—not one of those mini backyard kinds. Her back gate had a lock on it, a real lock, because her parents didn't let her leave the backyard on account of them thinking she could get kidnapped. That was the one thing that made my friendship with Annie different from my friendship with Tommy. Annie couldn't really have adventures like Tommy and me had.

"Hi Annie!" I said, and waved. She slowed down her swing and hopped off.

We sat on her front porch and she said, "Want to play a board game or something?"

"I'd love to swing," I said.

"I've been swinging for an hour. It's kind of boring."

"Not if you swing with another person," I said. "When we had a swing set, Bernadette and I used to have contests who could swing highest."

We went into her backyard and locked the gate behind us. Then we swung for about an hour and she got up so high the swing set jumped and she squealed a few times. I said, "You never swing highest by yourself, you know."

"That's deep, Obe."

"They call me the hippie."

"They call me putrid."

"You're not putrid."

I heard another gunshot as we swung, but I figured maybe people were setting off firecrackers or something. Then I saw a group of kids walking around THE ORCHARDS and I didn't think anything of it until I recognized Tommy, standing by himself on the corner, arms crossed, glaring at Annie and me swinging.

The first thing I thought was *Good. Let him be mad.*

The second thing I thought was how fun it was to swing and how not fun it was to walk around acting cool. Tommy must have seen me notice him, so he left. Then I heard another shot and I knew either Mike had his BB gun or they were setting off firecrackers on a boring Sunday afternoon. I was still happier to be on the swings with Annie. But I was worried too. If Mike could shoot his own brother in the foot, who knew what else he'd shoot at for a laugh?

I gave Annie the signal to slow down. I did a fancy jump once my swing was low enough. Annie tried the same but fell when she landed.

"You okay?" I asked.

"Just twisted my ankle a little bit."

"Annie, are you okay?" her mom said from the back sliding door.

"I'm fine, Mom."

"Come inside for a snack!"

Annie headed inside and I stopped and stared at the yard for a minute until I remembered. *Rubber pterodactyl, back right-hand corner.* They'd built a shed on top of it. Annie got lucky. That pterodactyl was one of my favorite toys when I was little. I was glad it was under her shed.

Annie's dad was baking snickerdoodle cookies and they smelled like the breakfast I'd skipped.

Annie showed me her rock collection. "And I got a tumbler!" she said, and brought out her rock tumbler. Annie's mom leaned over the table and dangled the necklace pendant Annie made from her first batch of polished rocks. Annie said, "It's calcite. From Mexico."

Mr. Bell said, "Anyone want a cookie?"

It was an hour and a half until Sunday dinner, but I was starving so I ate far too many snickerdoodles, which made my stomach feel weird but I didn't regret it.

"Wanna play Monopoly?" Annie asked.

"No, thanks."

"Oh."

"I'd play something else. It's just—uh—I play Monopoly a lot at home and I'm kind of sick of it."

"Uno?"

"Sure."

"Play to five hundred?"

I looked at the clock on their kitchen wall. "I have to be home in an hour."

We just played for fun and didn't score the games. The whole time I thought about my rubber pterodactyl. I used to bring it all the way out here before it was *Phase One*, before it was THE ORCHARDS, and Tommy and I would play dinosaur wars. We'd make mountains out of the dirt and valleys, and sometimes if it rained the dinosaurs would all drink from the puddles. I thought about telling Annie about Marvin too. She was my best friend but I don't think she knew it. And best friends should share stuff with each other, but I still wanted Marvin to myself. It felt wrong, but lately I was getting used to feeling wrong.

An hour passed. I said thank you to Mr. and Mrs. Bell and said good-bye to Annie and when I got to the front porch, I touched my fingers to my nose and saw blood. I rang their doorbell and Annie gave me a stack of tissues. Her mom tried to make a big deal out of my nosebleed and suggested that she should drive me home, but Annie told her I got them all the time.

CHAPTER 17

FAIR FIGHTS & SUCKER PUNCHES

There were memories.

Whenever someone cared about my nosebleeds, or cared about me having a nosebleed, it was awkward. I didn't want attention. I just felt like disappearing every time one happened.

It was a complete setup, the whole fight.

Phase Three had started and the only place left to hang out was our wild patch. Half woods, half weeds and creek. I liked to play in both places. I liked the woods because it was spooky in there sometimes. But then when Tommy's new friends started playing there, they'd tell me to leave, and I'd say that it was my land and they couldn't tell me to leave. I made three NO TRESPASSING signs and nailed them to the trees, but they kept playing there.

The next week, they made a sign that said NO HIPPIES ALLOWED and hung it on one of my nails and hung another one just like it right in the middle of my log bridge over the creek.

I never knew where was the safer place to be. If I heard them playing war in the woods, I'd sit by the creek. If I saw them by the creek, I'd go to the woods. Every time they saw me, they'd follow me to my safe place and ruin it.

This went on until late fall when Tommy said he had a solution to the problem. The idea was: They wanted the woods as their turf. The idea was: If we had a real fight about it, whoever won would get the woods. If I won, I'd have all the Devlin land. If I lost, they'd get the woods, but I'd still get the creek. Tommy said this was fair even though Mike said that they should get all the land if they won. Tommy explained that technically, this was all Devlin land and it was probably smarter just to try to get the woods.

I knew Tommy was nervous to fight me because neither of us had ever been in a fight before. He must have known I was nervous too. Mike was the referee, which if you ask me was pretty unfair, but he promised to be fair.

We agreed to meet at the creek after school. I did some lame stretches while Tommy did some lame stretches and we both pretended that we knew how to box. Then Mike called us over to where the fight would be. He said he had to lay out the rules.

He stood between us, a little to my right, and started saying some rules. I don't remember what he said. My body was in complete fear mode because I didn't want me and Tommy to be fighting. I remember thinking, while Mike talked, that I would be happy to give those suburban boys the woods. I loved the woods, but I'd rather have the creek. And Mike was still talking and had his hands on our chests to keep us separated a little and I was looking at Mike, trying to hear what he was saying, and that's when Tommy pulled back his arm and aimed for my face and punched me. Before Mike even got done with the rules, I was bleeding all over my fall coat. I was so stunned it never even occurred to me that sucker punching your opponent was definitely against the rules. But I never brought it up. It was the end of the turf war.

They got the woods.

I got the creek.

As I walked up Orchard Way with my nosebleed, I had all the questions I always had when my nose bled. Had they planned it that way? Had Mike taught Tommy how to sucker punch me? If I told my parents what really happened, would Dad go out and tell those boys to get off our land?

I knew he wouldn't.

I think that was the hardest thing about Dad. He talked a good talk, you know? He said, *Be fearless, daring, and brave. Stand up for yourself!* But he'd never actually stand up for himself. Or maybe that was the hardest thing about me. I never went back to Tommy and said it wasn't a fair fight. I never got over my embarrassment enough to stand up for myself and take my own land back.

I was still embarrassed about it then, walking up Orchard Way, as it started to drizzle.

CHAPTER 18

RAIN & SUNDAY DINNER

There was rain. I knew it was coming. Back when this was a field, I could smell it. Now it was more a feeling on my skin because the field smelled like houses and cars and people and . . . Marvin.

My nosebleed was over by the time I got into *Phase Two*. The snickerdoodles were still making my stomach turn. Not like Annie's dad cooked them wrong or anything, but too much of anything is never a good idea. As I got closer to *Phase Three* I smelled a familiar smell. Marvin's scat was sticking in the damp air like the snickerdoodles were sticking in my guts.

I know it's gross to think about looking at poop. People get all weirded out by it and that's why the suburban boys called me the hippie and stuff. But scat is a reliable tool in the practice of wildlife conservation. Does that make me sound like an expert? It's what they had written on the inside of the pocket guide. Anyway,

I went looking for Marvin's poop. It was only misty-drizzling and the bell hadn't rung yet. Mom always rang the bell a bunch of times for Sunday dinner.

After sniffing around for a while, I found Marvin's poop right on the asphalt of one of the side roads off Orchard Way, over toward the curb and near a drain grate. It was a small pile, gooey, and a mix of bright colors. Someone might find it if the rain didn't wash it away first. From the look of the sky, the rain was going to come down hard, so I didn't worry. But I wished Marvin hadn't been out pooping in the middle of the street on a Sunday afternoon. He usually pooped in his bathroom area between the creek and the woods.

When I got home a few minutes before two, I went to the upstairs bathroom and washed my face and gargled mouthwash because I'd gotten so close to Marvin's scat that I didn't think I'd ever get the burn out of my nose.

Even though we were all there, Mom went outside and rang the bell for dinner. Then we sat down at the table and got ready to eat. Mom said a prayer her family had been saying for more than a hundred years. One hundred years ago at this very dining room table, my great-grandfather sat down to eat his Sunday dinners. My great-grandmother rang that bell. This was something no developer or bulldozer could take away from us.

I served myself the biggest portion of mashed potatoes and gravy that I could get away with and then passed my plate to get it filled with other things.

"I don't want too many potatoes, Obe," Mom said.

I dished her just enough.

"I want a lot," Dad said.

I dished him a lot.

"I heard you were playing with Annie," Bernadette said. She said it in that way. You know the way. *I heard you were playing with a girl! You like a girl!*

I stopped and stared at her. "Annie's my friend," I said. "So what?"

"I was just kidding with you," she answered.

"Good," I said as I slopped her potatoes over the side of her plate. I knew Bernadette didn't like an untidy plate so I did it on purpose. "Oops. Sorry about that."

"I was hoping for a real game of Monopoly today," Dad said. "Long version. All four of us."

"Please, Dad," Bernadette said. "No."

"It'll be fun!" Mom said.

"You haven't had to play with him for the last few months, Mom. He's a horrible winner," Bernadette said.

"And I drink your pathetic tears!" Dad said. This made everyone laugh.

I said, "And he steals from the bank all the time!"

The laughing stopped.

"I do not!" he said.

"I was kidding," I said. "I thought we were joking around."

"I think he steals too," Bernadette said, still laughing.

"Stop saying I steal!"

"He used to cheat at games when he was a kid," Mom says. "That's what his brother told me before we got married."

Dad's face got red and he said, "Stop it!"

"Oh, Jay! We're just kidding around!" Mom said.

"If it's not funny, then it's not kidding."

"Here's something that isn't funny," Bernadette said. She waited a few seconds until everyone looked at her. "Plastics."

I remembered Dad's rant about plastics and nearly choked on my mouthful of food. Once I swallowed, I laughed so hard I almost peed my pants. Bernadette had laughing tears running down her cheeks.

Mom said, "I miss all the in-jokes with this night shift."

"And Monopoly," Dad said. "That's why the kids are so happy to play today, right, kids?"

It started to rain then. The kind of rain you can hear when it's not even hitting the windows. We all looked outside and Dad said, "I hope the basement doesn't flood."

Mom said, "Shoot. I was hoping to get out and weed the flower beds today."

Bernadette wiped the side of her plate for the third time to clean off the potatoes I'd slopped there.

•••

We played Monopoly. It was the best game of Monopoly Bernadette and I had ever played because Mom insisted on being the banker. The game took two and a half hours before we all got bored and Bernadette was winning by a big margin. She said, "I hate to do this while I'm winning, but I really have some homework to do and I know Obe must be bored."

Dad looked relieved. He only had the railroads and the two smallest monopolies and even though he'd finally traded me for Boardwalk, he couldn't afford to build hotels on it yet. As always, I collected as many properties as I could, but I didn't build any houses or hotels on them. I never won Monopoly.

The rain had stopped. The basement didn't flood, but the carpet did get wet in a few spots. We'd never had a leaky basement before the developers showed up. Mom said they messed up all the soil drainage when they dug up the old field.

Dad went downstairs with his wet-vac and Mom followed him, and I figured that was as good a time as any to go outside and hang out with Marvin Gardens, so I put on my rain boots and went to the creek. What I saw when I got close enough made me stop breathing.

CHAPTER 19

TOMMY & MARVIN GARDENS

There was shock. There was disappointment and something like grief.

Tommy was sitting on the muddy bank of the creek and talking to Marvin while he fed him the bag of plastic I left there when I went for my walk that morning.

It took me about thirty seconds to inhale. I wanted to curse. I wanted to yell. I wanted to do so many things. Mostly I wanted to sucker punch him in the nose and give him nosebleeds for six months. Nosebleeds with no warning. Middle of science class. Middle of lunch. Middle of swimming at the rec center, freaking out the lifeguard.

But what I said was "What are you doing here?"

"I thought you might need some help," he said.

"I don't need your help."

He looked down and said quietly, "I might need yours."

Tommy had been crying and he had dirt all over his face. His fancy sneakers were covered in mud. I knew his mom would kill him for that.

"What happened?"

He wiped snot on his sleeve and pretended he hadn't just been honest with me. "Can we talk about this guy?"

"Marvin Gardens," I said. "That's his name."

"Seriously?"

"Seriously."

"Where did he come from?" Tommy asked.

"My guess: He evolved because of this," I said, and spun around to show *Phases One through Three*.

"I saw him in the woods. He let me follow him here. I didn't think you'd let me come over. I wouldn't blame you."

"Where's Mike and the other guys? You're like a gang now. Like all six of you or whatever."

"They're always daring each other to do stuff and it's going too far."

"What now?"

"Girls. So stupid. I don't even care about girls. I mean, not like that. You know what I mean."

"What about girls?"

"They're making a list," Tommy said. I looked at him like I didn't know what he was talking about, because I didn't. "They're going to kiss as many girls as they can before the end of the school year."

I frowned. "So the list is a list of girls?"

He nodded.

"I don't understand why you'd need a list."

"It's stupid. I told you. I told them too. And Mike said I was being immature."

"So he dropped you."

"Told me I was a hippie and I belonged with the freak."

"I'm the freak, right?"

"You're the freak."

I stayed quiet. Tommy and I never really dared each other to do things. I knew other kids did that sometimes. Last month, a kid in my class got glue all over his butt because someone put it on his chair. The month before that, one of them stuck a Post-it Note to the back of the lunch checkout lady's shirt that said I SMELL BAD.

"You're not a freak, though," he said.

It almost seemed like the old Tommy — my best friend — was back. Half of me wanted this. The other half of me didn't trust him one bit.

I looked at Marvin Gardens. "He's the freak," I said.

"He fetches, you know," Tommy said.

"I taught him," I said, trying to keep every bad word inside my mouth because there was Tommy, on my turf, with my Marvin Gardens. Worse, Marvin didn't even come over to me or jump up and grin. He just sat in the fast-running stream and munched.

"Did you know he eats plastic?" Tommy asked.

"Yeah."

Marvin was making that horrific noise, chewing on my sour cream container.

"You can't tell anybody about him," I said.

"I won't."

"I'm serious."

"I won't tell anybody. I promise," he said.

"I don't know what to do with him."

"Have you smelled his poop yet?" he asked. "That's how I found him on the edge of the woods. He was pooping."

"I swear that stuff is more toxic than the stuff that comes out of the landfill." I laughed and felt like a traitor.

"It's blue," Tommy said.

I guessed Marvin had been eating the plumbing plastic again. "Only if he eats blue stuff."

"What is he?"

"I have no idea. I want to find out, but there's nothing on the Internet and it's not like I can ask Ms. G or anything."

"I could ask her," he said. Tommy had had a crush on Ms. G since the beginning of that school year. I was probably the only one who knew this, because having a crush on a sixty-year-old lady would be weird to most kids. Except Ms. G wasn't her age. Her brain was cute . . . if you thought about girls being cute. He said, "I think she'd really want to see him."

"You can't tell *anybody*. I told you."

"Okay."

We sat on the bank and Marvin walked up and sat between us and I petted his head while Tommy inspected his own mud-covered sneakers. I waited for Tommy to say he was sorry for punching me in the nose but he didn't. I waited for him to say something else about how he needed my help like he said when I got there, but he didn't say anything. I didn't ask him about why his face was dirty. I didn't ask why he'd been crying.

This was how it was going to be, I guessed.

CHAPTER 20

ONE HUNDRED YEARS AGO

One hundred years ago, my great-grandfather did what he could for money. He trapped wild animals on trap lines stretching from the orchard all the way to the river. His kids would collect the animals and skin them——a fine art——and then he would sell the prepared skins. Muskrats, mostly. Rarely a mink or a raccoon. Sometimes he'd get a nickel for a skin. Sometimes he'd get a dime. At home, my great-grandmother made all of her food from scratch, kept a large garden, and kept livestock so she could feed the family. There was a meat man who would come by every month, but she couldn't afford to buy things from him, and after the meat man told my grandmother—— then only a little girl——that one day there might be spaceships that could take us to the moon, my great-grandmother told him to stop coming around. "We don't need to fill the kids with crazy talk," she'd said. That's what my mom tells me. Either way, the trapping money went to whiskey. But dimes and nickels couldn't keep up with my great-grandfather's debt at Hannah's Bar. On May 21, 1916, he owed enough to mortgage forty more acres.

CHAPTER 21

MONDAYS & SECRETS

There were secrets. The problem with secrets was: I never knew when someone had one.

I didn't hear Marvin Gardens howling in the night and I didn't see him anywhere on my walk to the bus stop that morning. Ever since the night he went walking down toward the riverbank, I had a feeling he slept down there — safe and out of the way of the workmen and anyone else who might be dangerous to him. I had a feeling that even though he wasn't scared of me, or now, Tommy, he was probably scared of other people. And bulldozers. And cement trucks.

I wasn't scared to go to the bus stop for once, but I knew Tommy was. Since I never asked him what happened, I didn't know how bad the new boys had been to him. I just knew Tommy didn't cry much and he'd been crying the day before when I saw him and Marvin at the creek. I still didn't like that he knew about Marvin—I didn't trust Tommy enough to keep it to himself.

Since school had this crazy schedule for buses, the bus always came right on time. I didn't know how they did that. It seemed impossible for anything to be on time all the time, but the bus always was. The timetable was always specific when we got it in the mail in August. That year, it said our bus would come at 7:17 a.m. And it did. Every morning. On the nose.

I got to the bus stop at 7:15. Two minutes to spare. Tommy wasn't there.

"Where's your hippie friend?" Mike asked.

"Was he too scared to come to school because there are *girls* there?" someone else said.

"He doesn't like girls."

"Probably likes boys!"

I didn't answer because those boys were stupid. Tommy wasn't afraid of girls. He and I talked to girls all the time. Tommy even thought Bernadette was cool the same way I did.

I heard the bus turn the corner and I looked toward Tommy's house. There he was, jogging and trying to look cool when all over his face was nervous. Even his feet looked nervous in those new sneakers . . . which were pretty old by now, but washed clean of the mud from the day before.

He got on the bus last and that's when I realized he had a lot more to worry about than just standing around at a bus stop with boys who didn't like him anymore. He didn't have anywhere to sit.

Since Annie's bus stop was three bus stops from ours, Tommy sat with me, slightly out of breath and with even more nervous on his face.

"Hey," I said.

"Hey."

"Annie has to sit here," I said.

"She can sit with Mike," he said.

"It's too far back for her to walk with her cello."

"I'll hold her cello if she wants me to," Tommy said.

Tommy was clearly not thinking straight. The bus driver hadn't noticed that he was in the wrong seat yet, so we drove to the next stop. Mike and his friends weren't saying anything mean to Tommy. They were all huddled around Mike and an open spiral notebook.

Tommy whispered, "That's the list."

I didn't answer. Then the familiar feeling started inside my nose. I held my finger up to it and checked for blood and dug in my pocket for a tissue but there weren't any tissues so I sniffed hard and then pinched my nose shut. I nudged Tommy and pointed to my face so he might help me. He searched his pockets for tissues and found a used one, but it was dry and old, he said. It would do. I held it to my nose and knew Annie would have a tissue in her backpack because she always did.

Tommy whispered, "I think we should tell Ms. G about Marvin Gardens."

"No."

"It's Earth Month! It's perfect timing!" he whispered. People like Tommy only thought about ecology one month a year when Ms. G's pollution facts aired on the announcements at school.

I leaned over to Tommy, still with his dirty tissue shoved into my nostril. "You can't tell *anybody*. Okay?"

He said "Okay" but I didn't believe it for a second. His nervousness was running from his face over to mine. What replaced it was some sort of scheme. I knew Tommy's scheme face. I'd seen it my whole life.

I said, "If you get Marvin Gardens taken away from the creek and sent to some lab somewhere where he's locked up and poked with needles, I'll kill you."

"I won't. I swear. I promise," he said.

"Then why do you look like you're planning something?" I asked.

The bus stopped, and when Annie Bell walked on the bus and saw Tommy sitting next to me, she froze. I was the only friend Putrid Annie had on that bus. We both knew this.

Tommy stood up and let her sit in the seat. Then right as she was sitting down, he leaned in and kissed her. Right on the lips. Or the side of her lips. She screamed out and then Tommy ran back to sit with Mike and his new friends and I heard them laugh and say things like "You kissed Putrid Annie!" and "We knew you weren't a loser!" and things like that.

Annie started to cry. I didn't know what to say. Tommy was a bigger jerk than I already thought he was. I needed one of Annie's tissues, so I said, "Annie, can I borrow a tissue?"

She laughed a little through her tears. "You can have one. I don't want it back." She peeled off four tissues and folded them for me so I could wrap them over my nose and not look like a freak with a bloody tissue shoved in my nostril.

"I'm sorry Tommy did that," I said. "That's not right." I thought about how he'd told me about the list the day before at the creek. I thought about the day he sucker punched me. The two had something in common.

She blew her nose and said, "It's okay. I'm going to tell the principal."

"Good," I said.

"I thought you were his friend again."

"Nah," I said. I thought about if Bernadette got kissed without permission and how she'd feel about it, and how I'd want to punch a guy who did it right in the face. "If you need a witness, you can tell the principal I saw it."

She looked at me and smiled. She took some extra tissues and held them out to me. "You should clean yourself up when you get to school."

I looked back at Tommy sitting next to Mike and I saw they were all still leaning in, looking at Mike's list of girls. What a stupid game. Tommy looked up at me and winked. I didn't know what the wink was supposed to mean, but I think it meant that I should trust him. Except how could I ever trust him? Here I was, with a nosebleed because he punched me in the nose, sitting next to Annie, who he just kissed and made cry.

Truth is, I wasn't worried about Annie or the kiss or my nose. I was worried about Marvin Gardens and what Tommy was scheming to do with *him*. Everything got more complicated with secrets.

CHAPTER 22

OCEAN SOUP & THE KISSING INCIDENT

There was power. Boys needed power over girls as far as kids like Tommy and Mike were concerned. I didn't think that way at all. I didn't know if I was normal or if they were, but I knew I was right. Calling a girl names like Putrid or kissing her out of the blue like that—it all just showed how dumb we boys were, not how powerful. And it showed Annie was right about why they called her Putrid Annie. None of those boys were thinking for themselves and they were probably scared of her for being smart.

The pollution fact on the announcements that day was *It takes a plastic bottle five hundred years to decompose. Americans throw away 2.5 million of these bottles per hour. Think about getting a reusable water bottle!*

Per hour? That's what I kept asking myself. *Per hour?*

This is what I thought about during my math test.

I didn't remember one question from the test once I walked out of the room, and I knew I'd probably failed.

•••

The Kissing Incident earned Tommy a three-day suspension. I was called into the office before lunch and I told the principal what happened. I might have told him about the list and the other boys making the list. I might have told him that Tommy wasn't himself—that he was being a jerk so those boys would treat him better. I might have told him that something had happened over the weekend but I didn't know what it was, even though it left dirt and tears all over my former best friend's face.

Not only did Tommy get suspended for kissing Annie Bell without her permission, but those boys got called in one by one to talk about the list, and the school called their houses to talk to their parents.

At lunch, people talked.

No one could understand why Annie was so *crazy* about the "dumb" kiss. Girls, boys, they all weighed in on how Tommy shouldn't get in trouble for what he did. It was like I was the only person who was thinking right about this stuff. We all learned since kindergarten that we can't touch other people without permission—what changed now that we were in sixth grade? One kid said Annie should be flattered because she was putrid and I said, "That's it!" really loud and everyone looked at me. Then I said, "How would you like it if some guy walked up to you right now and just kissed you?"

The boys looked grossed out. The girls looked like they were actually thinking about it. None of them answered. I was kind of amazed that I'd raised my voice.

Tommy came to science class and sat in his usual seat. He would miss Tuesday through Thursday for his suspension. He didn't look at me but I didn't think about that at the time. Tommy hadn't looked at me in six months, so I didn't know how anything was supposed to be anymore.

When Ms. G started her lesson on ocean pollution and put a slide up on the smart board with a jar of gel suspending plastic confetti, Tommy raised his hand.

"What would happen if an animal showed up that could eat all that plastic?" Tommy asked.

My whole body went weak and I started sweating so much I felt my skin cells peel off. Did you know humans lose about eight hundred tiny flakes of skin every minute? Forty thousand per hour. I lost all forty thousand when I heard Tommy ask this question. They just slid off and stuck to the inside of my clothes.

"Actually, there are microbes in the ocean that are breaking down plastics already, Tommy. Great question."

"But what if it wasn't microbes?" Tommy asked. "What if there was, like, a dog or a cow or something that ate plastic before it got to the ocean?"

"That would be interesting, I guess," she answered. "But today we're discussing how we can manage our own trash in more beneficial ways so we can keep our oceans cleaner."

I turned around and glared at Tommy in a way that made him glare back at me.

A minute later I got a note. *Thanks for getting me suspended, hippie.*

I wrote back even though I knew I shouldn't have. *I didn't yet you suspended.*

He wrote back. *Mike's dud shoots groundhogs with his rifle. A real rifle. Say good-bye to Marvin Gardens.*

I stared at that note for a long time. I didn't know what to say. I didn't know why Tommy had turned on me and Marvin. I still didn't know for sure if him showing up at the creek on Sunday was all a setup. Kids do that, you know. They set traps for other kids to fall into. Happens all the time. Just like sucker punches.

•••

At dinner, Mom had already heard that Tommy was suspended. I don't know how moms find this stuff out, but she asked me what happened and I told her.

"Annie sits next to me on the bus and Tommy kissed her without her permission," I said.

"What's that mean?" Dad asked.

Bernadette said, "You guys are in sixth grade!"

Mom said, "Seems harmless to me."

I said, "If some guy did that to you at your job, would it be okay?"

Dad said, "Tommy's just a kid. He didn't think about it, probably."

"They've been planning it for a while," I answered. "They've been making a list."

Bernadette said, "I can't believe you two think kissing people without permission is okay. You're parents. What's wrong with you?"

"I don't like that tone," Dad said.

"Annie's in fifth grade. She's only ten," I said.

"Remember when that boy from your class kissed you at the pool that day, Bernadette? You were in maybe second grade. It was cute," Mom said.

"It wasn't cute. His name was Adam and he was a jerk and he only kissed me when I wasn't looking because then he could say he'd kissed a girl."

"Harmless," Dad said.

"Not harmless if it leads to boys thinking they can do stuff to girls without permission," Bernadette said.

"Yeah," I said.

"Let's stop talking about it," Mom said. Convenient for her considering she started the conversation. Nobody talked about me not joining summer baseball, and I was happy about that.

So we didn't talk about baseball. We didn't talk about kissing or Tommy getting suspended. We didn't talk about plastics or pollution. We just ate dinner and then Mom went to work and Dad went to change out of his work clothes, and I headed toward the creek.

Marvin Gardens was right there in my spot, waiting for me. I'd brought four different kinds of plastic with me. A milk jug cap, which so far was his favorite. A small piece of plastic siding from the scraps in *Phase Three*. A thin plastic lid from a fast-food soda cup, and a piece of that anti-erosion fencing that smelled like a new shower curtain. I always loved that smell.

I laid out the four pieces of plastic on the bank of the creek and told Marvin to stay. He stayed.

"So out of these four kinds of plastic, which one would you eat first?" I asked.

He looked at me. Stood still.

I said, "Come on!"

Marvin went straight for the anti-erosion fencing and chewed it quietly while making that purring noise he made. After that, he went for the milk jug cap. The cap was louder when he chewed it, but I could still hear him purring. He ate the small lid next, and then he sniffed at the house siding and moved it around with his nose a little but didn't eat it.

"Why not the siding, Marvin?"

He couldn't answer me, but he still wouldn't eat it. I had no idea what made it different from the rest, but he seemed to hate it the way I hate cauliflower or blue food.

As we sat and played for a while, he rolled onto his back and I rubbed his belly and I giggled because it was still slimy and I could tell he was having fun. I couldn't stop thinking about him being nice to Tommy, though. Did he let Tommy rub his belly too? Did he go to the woods now that he had a friend there? And if he did, what would happen to him now that Tommy was suspended?

"Marvin, you have to be careful around Tommy. He's not a real friend. He can be really mean, and today he said he would hurt you."

Marvin just grinned at me and then jumped down and rolled around in the creek. I guess animals don't have real meanness and can't understand it. They just live and eat and poop and sleep and even though they have personalities and seem mean sometimes, it's all inborn and not thought-out, like Tommy thought out that note to me about Mike's dad.

And who shoots groundhogs in the suburbs, anyway?

I never saw Marvin Gardens be mean. His personality was food-centered, but I didn't know if he was hungry all the time or just lonely or sad or lost. Kind of like me. Maybe sometimes it took a while to find your personality. Maybe it was okay that I didn't know what I wanted to do with my life, my feelings, with Tommy, or with what happened to Annie Bell. Maybe my dad made it more complicated by telling me I wasn't supposed to have feelings because I was a boy. Maybe he didn't have a personality because he was messed up too.

Marvin Gardens, in one short week, had become my pet, my companion, my best friend. He had been a traitor when he let Tommy feed him, but I didn't want to see him that way. Now he was someone to be protected the way the government protects owls and bats. I didn't know if Tommy was serious about Mike's dad and his gun. I didn't know anything. And neither did Marvin.

CHAPTER 23

ONE HUNDRED YEARS AGO

One hundred years ago, my great-grandmother's relatives came to family picnics on the old farm homestead and slipped spare change into her apron pockets. She never served beer at picnics— only lemonade and iced tea. When my great-grandfather would leave for the bar, she'd hand all the spare change to my grandmother, who knew to bury the change somewhere my great-grandfather couldn't find it. Money for food. Money for emergencies. World War I was raging and nothing was easy. It's not like my great-grandmother was ever going to wear anything fancy outside of her funeral dress. The money was for butter and thread and sometimes she had to pay the doctor for *accidents* that happened to her because her husband had a *problem*. One hundred years ago, my great-grandfather came home from Hannah's Bar and a family picnic was still in full swing. He brought out his gun and was showing off when he shot one of his workhorses by accident. He didn't have the money to buy another horse, so he went to the bank and got a loan to buy a new thing called a tractor. He put up sixty-five more acres for the money. The bank knew he couldn't afford the new loan or the old mortgage, but they let him do it anyway.

CHAPTER 24

THE FORT & TOXIC WASTE

There were sides. You had to take one. If you didn't, people thought you were weak. I didn't ever have a side, so I was weak. But when I reported the truth about The Kissing Incident to the principal, I took a side. It was the right side, but everyone on every side thinks they're on the right side once they take a side. No matter if you're wrong, it's hard not to be loyal to the side you picked.

I know this sounds weird, but I'd rather be loyal to myself than to a bunch of guys who made fun of my old sneakers. Maybe I didn't mind being alone. Maybe I didn't care about having friends until I found one who was as loyal to me as I was to myself.

Marvin was an animal and not a human being. He was loyal to everyone, including Tommy, not just me. Maybe Tommy needed him two days ago as much as I did. Maybe Tommy didn't want to kiss Annie Bell on the bus but something else made him do it.

The whole thing made me want to cry.

And crying wasn't allowed.

Marvin went toward the river clicking and talking to whoever he knew down there. I stayed by the creek facing the woods. The woods were quiet because the boys were at baseball practice. I realized baseball practice meant I could go into the woods and not get caught.

The new kids had been bragging that they'd made a fort there since spring started. I found it. It wasn't a very good fort. It didn't have a roof or anything. They'd just dragged logs into a square and then stacked up other logs so they had walls that came up to my knees. It didn't even have a doorway. I had to climb over the logs to get into the fort.

Inside the fort there was an old Styrofoam cooler, the kind people used at summer picnics or as a place to store bait if they were going fishing in the river. The cooler held a two-liter bottle of birch beer, a slingshot, a catalog that had pictures of ladies in underwear, and a bag of assorted candy.

I walked out of the fort and back to my old favorite tree. In a patch of mostly fir trees there were a few deciduous trees, and my favorite was the maple, because in the fall I could see it turn colors from our upstairs bathroom window. When I got to the maple, I saw a pile of something over near where the creek passed by the woods so I went to it. It was a pile of trash. Plastic trash. I knew it was Tommy's because it had a bunch of empty bottles of

Gatorade—the blue kind that I refused to drink on account of it being blue. It looked like they'd only put the pile there recently, no doubt to lure Marvin Gardens onto their turf.

I didn't want to think about Tommy telling his new friends about Marvin. I guess I knew deep down that he'd told them. But I still hoped he hadn't.

I walked over to the pile of plastic. When I got close enough, I saw a rope that went from the floor of the woods to high up in a tree. The rope was taut, like there was something hanging on it. I stopped and looked up for a long time but I couldn't see where the rope started in the tree. This was some sort of trap, but I didn't know what kind.

I looked around for a long branch—not hard to find in the woods—and I picked it up. I stood as far away from the trash as I could and I hit the rope. Something raced down through the trees and hit the pile of trash right in the middle with a loud thud.

Someone had whittled a branch into a pointed tip. A spear. Someone had set it up so if Marvin came to eat the trash, he'd get skewered by the branch.

I stood there staring for a minute. Steaming mad, but I didn't know what to do about it.

I looked around for other traps, other ropes, other piles of bait. All I found was a sort of old-style rabbit trap—a big milk crate balanced on a stick with a plastic bottle placed under it. The crate was too small to contain Marvin anyway. I left it untouched and walked out of the woods, feeling a million times more angry than I'd been in a long time.

Even during the sucker punch, I hadn't felt angry — I'd felt embarrassed. Even when I found Tommy with Marvin at the creek, I'd felt conflicted, not angry. Now my brain thought of a hundred things I could do to trap those boys the way they wanted to trap Marvin. I went back to the fort and opened the cooler. I emptied the birch beer onto the ground and hoped a million ants would come to drink it. I ripped the sling off the slingshot and put it in my pocket. I jumped on the bag of candy until it was a mash of chocolate and wrappers and goo.

I was choosing a side.

As I walked from the woods to the creek, I tried to feel bad for what I'd just done, but couldn't. How could Tommy get in with a bunch of boys who wanted to trap an innocent animal? His mom rescued their two dogs from a shelter and had a bumper sticker that said RESCUED IS MY FAVORITE BREED. Up until six months ago, Tommy loved animals. I know that because we loved them together. Now he wanted to kill Marvin Gardens because of Mike, presumably — Mike who made his little brother take off his shoe and sock anytime Mike said so to show off his BB. I walked toward the creek. I threw the rubber sling from the slingshot as far as I could toward the train tracks.

I noticed hollowed-out pits in the high grass between the woods and the creek. They were about six inches deep and a foot or more wide and the grass around the pits was dead almost a whole foot away from the pit.

And there was that smell.

When I looked closely, I could see what caused it. It was Marvin's scat. It ate away at the ground and ate away the life around it. It looked like the pictures I'd seen of toxic waste and how it bubbles into the dirt and ruins it forever. This was Marvin's bathroom. Around me were at least ten of these pits.

My anger turned to fear. My fear turned to worry.

I ran home and actually did my math homework.

CHAPTER 25

SUSPENSION & SCAT CIRCLES

There were people who believed aliens made circles with their flying saucers in fields. They called these crop circles, and there was a lot of information on the Internet about this. Of course, people who believed in aliens were like people who believed in Bigfoot. Like me—a boy with a secret animal.

The Internet didn't tell me anything about scat circles. I looked at pictures of toxic waste and none of it was like Marvin's bathroom. I thought about telling Mom or Bernadette or Annie but I didn't want to tell anyone. Marvin was my secret.

Tommy's suspension from school made me nervous. Every day I was in school and he wasn't he could be finding Marvin. Talking to him. Feeding him. Trapping him. Maybe even killing him. I didn't think Tommy had the ability to kill an animal. I didn't think wearing the right kind of sneakers could turn a boy into a killer, but you never knew what those boys were saying to him.

On Tuesday people were still talking about The Kissing Incident. There were debates at the lunch tables and girls were starting to stick up for Annie. By Wednesday at lunch, they'd heard about the list from somewhere — I swear I didn't tell them. But someone did. They were avoiding all the boys in Tommy and Mike's group so they wouldn't have the same thing happen to them.

Wednesday's morning announcement fact was brutal. *Every ninety seconds, a child dies from contaminated water.* There was no positive to offer after this fact. Nothing we, as students in an elementary school, could do would help this. Ms. G was out sick on Tuesday and Wednesday, and the substitute wasn't anything like her. He liked to stand in the back of the room in the corner and watch us fill out work sheet packets about the environment. I don't think he even liked kids . . . or science. At the end of class on Wednesday he said, "Earth has been here for four-point-five billion years. It knows what it's doing. It knows how to clean itself — like a cat knows how to clean itself."

He overlooked the fact that if the Earth was really a cat, then we'd have to pretend that the cat was being followed by humans who were pouring dangerous chemicals onto it and making it breathe nasty air and drink contaminated water day in and day out. Would the cat still just lick itself clean every day and be fine or would it get sick?

That's what I wanted to say to him. But I just finished my work sheets.

On Wednesday the bus was mayhem. Tommy still wasn't there but Mike and the other boys wouldn't sit down, wouldn't stop yelling, and wouldn't stop taunting Annie. *Rats get trapped! Putrid Annie likes girls! Watch out, I have a BB gun and I know how to use it!* I wondered how Mike's little brother felt about that last one. I'm not sure shooting your brother by accident amounted to "knowing how to use it."

The bus driver yelled a lot. Annie ignored all of it. She had this smile on her face that I'd never seen before. It was a scheme smile.

"What's going on, Annie?" I asked.

"Look what I got." She pulled out a phone — a smartphone like the kind Bernadette had.

"That's awesome! I'm not allowed to have one of those until I'm in high school."

"My parents think it will keep me safe when I'm away from home."

I thought about the last thing she said. "Does this mean you're allowed to come to the creek with me after school?"

"The creek?"

"My creek. Where I get you the rocks. I've always wanted to show it to you but it was too cold when you moved here."

"I still have to stay home after school," Annie said. But she still had that smile.

I was smiling too. I couldn't hold Marvin in anymore. There wasn't enough room inside me. "Think about it. I have something I really want to show you. It's pretty important."

"Do those jerks hang out at the creek too?"

"Nope."

She looked at her new phone. She tapped on the screen and looked at a calendar. "Mom and Dad work until six tomorrow."

"Maybe tomorrow, then. You won't regret it," I said.

She still had that smile as she said good-bye at her stop and got off the bus. She was smiling so big I don't think she heard Mike and his friends saying stuff to her. *Stay Putrid!*

After school I went out to the creek and Marvin still wasn't there. I'd left some recycling for him on Tuesday and it was gone, so I saw this as a good sign, but maybe someone else took it. Maybe Tommy was collecting it during his suspension days off. Maybe he was building another trap.

I looked for new scat but couldn't find any. I went to the sites of the old scat, though, and the dead grass circles around them seemed to be growing. The pits looked deeper too. I stuck my nose into my sweatshirt to block the smell and went to the creek bed to grab some rocks. I put the rocks on the outsides of the scat circles to mark the edges. The whole thing scared me. The scat was growing toxic circles on my land—on Devlin land. So near the creek—only three stops from the Atlantic Ocean. And no sign of Marvin anywhere.

I was so freaked out I had a bad dream on Wednesday night. This grayish-brown Play-Doh was chasing me through the old field. The corn leaves were cutting my face as I ran. The ground was slippery like it had rained and I worked hard to keep my footing. In the dream, I knew that Marvin was dead, and when I woke up, I woke up with a scream.

On the bus, Annie sat down and said hello. I was still thinking about my dream.

"You okay?" she asked.

"Tired. Had a weird dream."

"Was it scary?"

"Yeah."

"I hate those."

"Yeah," I said.

"Have you seen Tommy?" she asked.

"Nah. I guess we'll see him tomorrow morning."

"He's a jerk," she said.

"Yeah."

"Are you sure you're okay?"

"I'm fine."

"You don't seem like yourself."

Thursday's announcement fact was: *Millions of people in America suffer from noise pollution, which causes hearing loss, sleep problems, high blood pressure, higher stress, and lower productivity.* I knew plenty about it already. *New Spacious Homes!* can teach a kid a lot about noise pollution. Loud machinery, lots of truck traffic, and the sound of a hundred hammers and nail guns was no different from what people who lived near airports or busy train routes had to endure.

Maybe all that noise was what drove Tommy to ask his mom to buy those sneakers. Being called names by the new kids could be a type of noise pollution. Maybe it was the type that pushed a kid over the edge — because Tommy had to have been pushed over an edge to be acting like he did for the last six months.

And anyway — what was noise pollution compared to Marvin's scat? That stuff was eating holes in the ground and killing everything it touched. I tried not to think about it, but it was all I thought about. I once thought Marvin could be the pollution solution, but now he could be part of the problem.

When I met Annie on the bus home I said, "Sorry I've been acting weird."

She said, "Okay."

"Are you coming to the creek with me today?"

"I don't know," she answered. "I could get in big trouble."

"I promise, it will be so worth it." When I said this, I hoped Marvin was back. It would be a bad idea to get Annie in trouble when she couldn't even meet Marvin.

"Maybe tomorrow. My parents just gave me the phone and . . . I don't feel right about what happened on Monday yet."

"It wasn't your fault," I said.

"Yeah, but I'm still embarrassed. And Tommy got suspended and it feels like my fault."

"Tommy's a jerk. He got suspended because he's a jerk."

"Still embarrassing, though. Like — why *me*, you know?"

I smiled at Annie until she found a smile to give back to me. I wanted to say something more, but then we both started laughing for no real reason. Just goofy.

I wanted to tell her about Marvin. But not on the bus with all those jerks. Maybe I could just show him to her. Tomorrow, if I could find him. So we goofy-laughed all the way to her stop and I felt better about pretty much everything for those ten minutes.

CHAPTER 26

TRUTHING & DARING

There was truth. The truth was: Marvin's scat wasn't right. The pits were growing. The rocks I'd put on the rim on Wednesday were at least two inches inside the holes by Thursday.

The truth was: I had to find Marvin soon.

He'd been gone for four days and I didn't believe Tommy or his new friends had killed him. Marvin was smarter than to fall for a few old dumb trap ideas. The answer was down by the river and I knew it. I wasn't allowed past the train tracks — I knew that too. But I thought fearless, daring, brave boys should break rules.

I walked from Marvin's bathroom through *Phase Three* toward the river. The workmen had all gone home but I could see they'd been digging out stumps, fixing the bank to Gilbrand Road, and marking out lots. The lots by the river were the biggest lots, which meant bigger *New Spacious Homes!* would drown in the next big hurricane. Not like I wished that on anyone, but it just seemed stupid that people would build a house on a floodplain. Crops loved floodplains. Houses, not so much.

The workmen had carved out a new road down by the last batch of lots on *Phase Three*. It was one of those loop roads—it would only take you to those houses and then come back up to the main road again. I imagined the road would be called Drowning House Road. That's what I would call it, anyway.

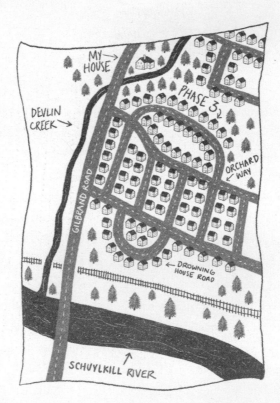

I walked on the train tracks for about a hundred yards because it felt fearless and daring and brave and I knew the train didn't come very often, and when it did, it blew its horn. Then that familiar smell wafted up and I looked around for a scat circle. It was ten feet from the tracks on the river side. It wasn't a sunken pit, though. It was fresh scat.

Today's poop cache was fluorescent orange—the same color as the anti-erosion fencing. Marvin's candy.

As I approached the riverbank I got nervous. It was a steep slope. By the road, which was the only place I ever approached the river from before, it was steep but graded so people could bring their canoes or something. This slope was natural. No one had made it easy for humans. I sat down and pondered my options. I only had one. I'd have to slink down on my butt through the brush, which seemed like it would be painful. If I lost my footing, I'd either slam into a tree trunk or end up in the fast, wide Schuylkill River. And I wasn't a very good swimmer.

I stayed on the edge of the steep bank for a while. I wondered what it must have been like to be my great-grandfather. Maybe he sat on this very spot once. Maybe my grandmother did. Maybe my mother. Maybe five hundred years ago a Lenape kid sat here and watched the sun rise.

I started slinking down the hill—one hand behind me to keep me balanced, the other out front. I didn't look down. I figured that was the easiest way to fall. I felt thorns and scrapes and prickly things along my legs but I kept going. I wasn't even sure why. Marvin could be up at the creek. Or he could be in the woods, eating the food near the traps the new boys had left for him.

If it wasn't so steep, this would have been a great place to live. The view of the river was pretty. The mountain behind it, the bridge to the right — it was the perfect place to have a deck. If this was still our land, I'd ask Mom if I could have this riverbank and I'd design a house on stilts and I wouldn't cut down any of the trees around it. It would be like a giant fort. A giant fort waiting to drown in the next hurricane, but still, I would know the risk going into the project.

I slid down another ten feet and stopped when I saw something bright to my right. Down by the riverbank, there was a large boat or something. It was colorful and near the water, so I aimed myself to the right and kept scooching down. It was like moving horizontally on a skyscraper. The more I stared at the boat, the more I knew it wasn't a boat. The closer I got to it, the less fearless, daring, and brave I felt. My imagination made the boat into a tent. Inside the tent lived a man who would kill me. That sort of thing.

I kept thinking scary stuff until I got close enough to see what it was. It was a huge roll of anti-erosion fence. Fluorescent orange. The same color as Marvin's scat. Either the workmen lost it over the bank or . . . Marvin Gardens was as smart as I thought he was.

The riverbank was Marvin's home, for sure. And that roll of anti-erosion fencing was like his refrigerator. Better, even. It was like breakfast in bed.

The sky was getting dark. Clouds moved in. It was a school night. I felt less fearless, daring, and brave when I thought about what time it might be.

I climbed back up the hill and jogged down the train tracks. As I neared *Phase Three* I heard someone call out, "Hey kid!" I stopped and looked over to one of the new lots, where there was this guy standing next to a pickup truck.

"Come here!" he yelled.

I knew not to talk to strangers, but this guy seemed okay. He was looking down at the dirt and had a flashlight even though it wasn't completely dark.

I walked to him and saw he had on construction clothes.

"Do you work here?" I asked.

"I came back for my phone." He held up his phone.

"Oh," I said.

"You're the kid who lives up there, right?" He looked me up and down.

"Yeah."

"You see any more of these around?" he said, and pointed his flashlight toward the piece of ground he'd been looking at. It was a small scat circle — no bigger than a salad plate — with Marvin's poop still visible in the middle. Bright orange.

I leaned in to see it. "Ugh! That smells gross!" I said. "What do you think it is?"

"Looks like . . . um . . . crap to me. Never saw anything like it, though."

"Me neither. Maybe it's something weird that's happening because you're building houses on sacred land."

He looked at me funny then. I don't know why I said it. I didn't know if it was real sacred land, but it was sacred to me.

"Whatever it is, the boss won't like it if it keeps leaving a mess like this on the site."

Talk about irony. The whole site was a mess. Their mess. *Phase Three.*

I walked back to the creek and waited until the guy's truck drove up Gilbrand Road. Then I ran to the back porch and grabbed my trowel and went back to the circle the guy showed me and removed Marvin's scat. I covered the circle up with dirt. I hoped the remaining scat wouldn't eat through the dirt, but it was the best I could do. I washed off the trowel in the creek and walked through the wild patch home.

The truth was, Marvin pooping out in *Phase Three* was dangerous. The truth was, I didn't know what to do about the scat.

CHAPTER 27

FAKING & SNEAKING

There were okay lies to tell if they were worth telling, and sometimes fearless, daring, and brave boys told the lies they had to tell. I stayed in bed long enough to know I'd miss the bus, then I told Mom I overslept. She drove me to school. I got to avoid Tommy on the bus.

The pollution fact of the day was: *More than one million plastic bags are used every minute. You can help change this by using reusable fabric shopping bags. Did you know that several countries have already banned plastic bags completely?*

I'd been trying to tell Mom and Dad to buy reusable bags for two years, but they always had a reason not to. Mom said that she always reused the plastic bags. What she didn't say is that she reused them and then threw them in the trash, which put them in a landfill, which didn't help the problem. Dad said things like,

"Why should I spend a dollar on a reusable bag I'll always forget at home when I get the plastic ones for free?" See also: *Blah blah blah blah blah.*

No one was talking about The Kissing Incident anymore. I knew Annie was still thinking about it and I knew I was still thinking about it, but school had moved on to other topics. Mostly, it was Friday and everyone likes Fridays.

On the bus home, Annie seemed all mixed up. Part sad and part happy. She had a book out of her backpack and said, "I'm loving this book!" but I could tell she wasn't reading the words. Her eyes just sort of blanked out on the pages. She looked nervous.

"Are you sure you're okay?" I whispered.

"Yeah."

"Still coming with me today, right?"

"I have to drop my stuff off at home. And get something. Um — I . . ."

When her stop came, I walked off the bus behind her.

"You didn't have to come with me," she said.

"I didn't want you to be walking alone."

"That's nice." She said that, but she didn't sound like she meant it.

"You're sure you're okay?" I asked as we stepped up to her front porch.

"Fine."

"You seem scared," I said. "I can just go home if you want."

"It's fine. Just let me drop this off." I expected to follow her into her house because that made a lot of sense to me, but then when she opened the door, she closed it right behind her. "I can't have you in after school. It's the rules," she said through the door.

"I'll just go home," I said. "I can show you the thing I wanted to show you another time. I know you're having a hard week."

"No!" she said. "I'll be out in a minute. Wait there."

When she came out, she looked more nervous than she had before. "I don't want anyone to see me." She had a hooded sweatshirt on and she pulled the hood over her head.

"This way," I said, cutting through two yards on the opposite side of Orchard Way to the dismal planet that was the untouched part of *Phase Three*. "We'll be back here so no one will know."

As we walked alongside the railroad track, Annie started picking up rocks and putting them in her sweatshirt pocket. She said things like "Diabase! That's Jurassic!" She held up a different rock she found around the tracks. "This one could be more than five hundred and seventy million years old!" She still looked nervous and I was starting to feel nervous too, because I was about to finally let my secret out.

I stopped walking and said, "I have to tell you something."

This made her look even more nervous. She took out her phone and checked the time. She said, "We've already been gone ten minutes."

"I discovered an animal. I mean, a brand-new kind of animal." Now she looked at me in a weird way. "Stop looking at me like I just told you I found Bigfoot."

"Are you serious?"

"Totally serious," I said.

"What kind of animal?" she asked.

"Hard to explain. It's a sort of mix between a hog and a dog and a peccary and probably some other stuff thrown in. I can't find it anywhere on the Internet. It's smart and can understand basic commands. But it . . . um . . . eats plastic."

Annie started laughing.

"I'm serious," I said.

She kept laughing. I felt relief even though she was laughing at me.

"Don't laugh. Even Tommy saw it. He even saw it eating plastic."

This made her stop laughing. "You're friends with Tommy?"

"Nah. He just likes to trespass and I found him with the animal last weekend. It's real, Annie. I'm not kidding around."

"Let's go, then," she said. "I only have an hour and a half."

When we got to the creek, I was happy to find Marvin was sloshing around in the water.

I said, "Marvin!" He turned and ran toward us. Annie stopped walking. I leaned down and rubbed Marvin on his head. "You've been gone for days, buddy. I was worried about you."

Marvin walked over to Annie and she didn't move at all. She didn't seem scared—just confused.

"Annie, this is Marvin. Marvin, this is Annie," I said.

"Marvin," Annie said.

"Marvin Gardens. It's a long story."

"Can I touch him?"

"He doesn't bite." I took out two milk caps from my pocket. "Watch your ears, though. This part can get noisy."

CREWAHARKKKLTKELTH!

Annie put her hands over her ears at first and then leaned down to pat Marvin on his head. "I get it. Marvin Gardens. Ironic!"

This is why Annie Bell would always be my friend. In one short minute, she knew what Marvin meant to me. She didn't have a problem touching a slimy impossible animal. She knew what irony was.

"Wow, Obe."

"Yeah."

"He's incredible."

"I know. Look at his feet!" I pointed to his feet.

"What *is* he?"

I shrugged. "I looked everywhere to figure it out. He doesn't exist. I mean, he does, but he doesn't. You know?"

Annie kept patting and petting Marvin's head. It made me happier than I thought it would. I thought if I shared him, he wouldn't belong just to me anymore. But now he belonged to both of us and it made me feel lighter. He stood there kind of purring and clicking at the same time. "How long have you known about him?" Annie asked.

"A week or two now. I found him in the creek. But I'm pretty sure his house is down by the river."

She looked at him closely and said, "I don't know a lot about animals, but I don't think I've ever seen anything like this before."

"He's brand-new. Or maybe he walked here from somewhere else. I don't know."

"His skin, though. He's like an amphibious mammal or something."

133

"I know. I can't tell what sort of mixed-up thing he is, but he's ours." *Ours.*

I walked Annie to the creek and Marvin jumped in and splashed around. We sat on the log bridge and watched.

"You really okay, Annie? I know if that kissing thing happened to me, I'd still be mad," I said. I didn't tell her I'd be scared too, but I would be.

"No one said anything to me today in school about it. I guess I'm okay. Thanks for asking, though. Even my parents stopped caring by yesterday." She let some time pass. Then she said, "I am still mad, though."

Annie jumped down from the bridge and onto the bank. She squatted down and started digging around for rocks. She pulled a few out, washed them in the creek, and put them in her pockets. Marvin watched her do this for a while. I did too. Then Marvin started digging his nose into the creek bed and pulling rocks out for her. She washed them in the creek and put them in her pocket with the other ones.

"I should go soon," she said. She stood up and climbed the shallow bank and brushed off her jeans, which were way muddier than they should be for a girl who went home and didn't leave.

"I'll walk you to the edge of Phase Three," I said.

Marvin shook the water off and then followed us. He made a noise like he was sad Annie was leaving and she stopped to rub his head again.

"Thanks for telling me about him," she said.

"Thanks for not thinking I was crazy."

She fumbled with something in her pocket and brought out her phone. "Can I take a picture of him?"

Right then there was a loud whirring noise of a revving engine, and I saw the pickup truck from the night before parked up by Orchard Way. The construction site was empty. The guy pointed at me and yelled, "Hey kid!" and without a word, Marvin sprinted toward the woods and Annie Bell sprinted down the tree line.

I yelled to Annie, "Call me when you get home safe!" I don't know if she heard me.

The pickup truck man walked toward me. "Did you forget your phone again?" I asked.

"I'm on vandal watch," he said. "Have you seen anyone messing with the houses or the equipment?"

Everything had changed so quickly. Annie knew Marvin. Marvin was gone, probably running toward his house. I let the guy's question float around until I could piece it together. "Someone's hurting the equipment?"

"Paintballs."

I didn't know what he meant. "Paint . . . balls?"

"Kids, probably. Get a paintball gun, and what else is there to shoot around here?"

I thought about it for a minute. "Is that why you were here last night? That thing you showed me?" Man, I was good at playing stupid.

"That wasn't paint," he said.

"Oh."

"So you don't know anyone with a paintball gun?"

"I never even knew there were such things as paintballs until a minute ago."

"Keep your eyes open for me, yeah? If you see anything weird, my name's Doug. Okay?"

"Okay."

"And if this is your handiwork, you better cut it out quick," he said.

CHAPTER 28

DIRTY SNEAKERS & MELTING FLOORS

There were five boys who came home in dirty sneakers right before dinner on a Saturday night. It would have been four boys except Dylan brought his little brother with him. I overheard them on the bus Monday morning.

"By yesterday afternoon, the soles of my sneakers were just gone," Mike said.

"Mine too," Tommy said.

"My mom said she was gonna kill me for what I did to the kitchen floor."

"You should see the holes in our deck. Something ate right through it."

Then Tommy's voice again. "I think I know who did this."

I could feel them all staring at the back of my head. Annie looked at me like she could feel it too.

"My dad called the cops this morning," one of the boys said. "He was afraid to touch the stuff. I saw it bubbling."

"It's, like, acid or something."

"The cops will arrest whoever did it," Tommy said.

He said it loud right at me. I could still feel his stare. Except I had no idea what they were talking about. Well, I had *some* idea, but I wasn't sure. I knew Tommy must be furious that his Mike-impressing sneakers had been ruined. I knew Tommy's parents. They wouldn't go buying him a new pair if he ruined the first pair. It didn't make sense that they were blaming it on me, but one hundred years ago, people blamed other people for no reason at all too.

"What are they talking about?" Annie asked.

"I don't know."

"Sorry I didn't call you on Friday to let you know I got home okay," she said.

"I didn't think you heard me."

"How's Marvin?"

"Fine, I guess." I wanted to say *still pooping toxic waste* but I didn't want Annie to know about Marvin's bad side yet. "Thanks for coming with me on Friday. I'm so glad you got to meet him."

"I want to go down to the river to see his house . . . or den or whatever," she said. "My parents didn't know I was gone on Friday, so I was thinking maybe today I could come over again."

"You should. We could walk down. I can tell you some other stuff about Marvin," I said.

"I'll meet you at the creek at four."

I didn't answer because I was distracted. The boys kept talking about how the police were going to arrest a kid who poured acid on their decks and sneakers and stuff. So stupid. Like anyone would go around with acid, ruining sneakers.

"You look pale," Annie said.

"I feel funny," I said.

"Please don't throw up on me."

I smiled. And then the feeling came in my nose. Annie knew what to do. She got out four tissues and folded them twice and gave them to me. Annie Bell was my nosebleed hero.

This nosebleed didn't stop. I was sent to the nurse after homeroom and she made me lie down and that usually helped, but this time, it didn't. It was a gusher.

The Earth Month fact of the day on the announcements was: *Lake Karachay, in Russia, is the most polluted spot on Earth. The lake is so radioactive it could kill a child who stands near it for five minutes. Learn more about pollution and conservation in the library! Ms. M has all the books you need!*

The nurse kept checking on me and looking at the bloody tissues in the trash can and sighing. Sometimes she yelled at kids with headaches to test to see if they really had a headache. She wasn't the nicest nurse on the planet.

As I lay there, I thought about what the boys on the bus were talking about that morning. Holes in their decks and steps? Ruined sneakers? It had to be Marvin's scat. They must have walked through his bathroom and tracked the stuff home. Which meant their parents would soon figure everything out, and I had to do something.

I don't know why Tommy thought I was somehow behind all of it. He knew me once. It wasn't like I was the one who'd changed. Even though I'd done what I did to their fort, I was still Creek Boy. The hippie. The freak. The kid who still didn't care about what kind of sneakers I wore.

People are really weird. They just think you should be like them, pretty much. Dad thought I should be like him. Tommy thought I should be like *him*. I just wanted to be me. And I wanted my field back. And I wanted to save Marvin Gardens before Tommy's boys trapped him or worse.

Lying there on the nurse's cot, I realized that I could do some of this stuff, but I couldn't do others. Namely, I could be me and I could save Marvin, maybe. But I could never get my field back. I don't know why it took three phases of developments for me to see it this clearly, but on that cot, on that day, I saw it and I took it in, and for the first time since *Phase One*, I cried about it. I wasn't thinking about Tommy or the police or the melting stuff or Marvin or Lake Karachay or anything else. I pictured everything the field once was — the spring fertilizer and plows, the summer corn and the way we'd measure how tall it was every week like some sort of seasonal clock, the harvest machines in autumn, and sledding down the hill toward the river in winter, dried stalks sticking out from the snow. None of it would ever happen again and I knew it.

I lay there on the nurse's cot sobbing. Once I started, I couldn't stop. I made sure to be quiet so the nurse wouldn't hear me. But I cried so hard, I made my nose gush blood. It took me a few minutes to make myself feel better.

When I grow up, I can buy my own field. It'll be Devlin's field because it'll be mine. Until then, I just have to get by.

I cleaned up my tears and knew they'd still show. I didn't care. I heard classes moving in the hallway so I'd been in the nurse's office more than an hour. She came into the little area where my cot was, checked the tissue on my nose, and said, "Okay, I'm going to send you home now. This one is stubborn. You need to see a doctor. They'll probably cauterize it for you."

"Cauterize it?"

"It's just a thing they put up your nose to fix the vein that's weak. It's easy now. Back in my day it was like a soldering iron. Hot poker. Up your nose. Not pretty." She said this in a voice like a backhoe. "My little sister got it done. Smelled like burning flesh." She had to add that. I'm not sure why. "I'm going to call your mom now, okay?"

I nodded and she went to her nurse desk and called my mom. Twenty minutes later, I was in the car, nose still gushing. Mom talked about what the nurse said to her about getting my nose cauterized and having to make a doctor's appointment for me.

After a few minutes of silence, she said, "Do you know anything about the vandals who went around the neighborhood last night?"

"I'm not sure I know what a vandal is," I lied. Doug the pickup truck guy had made it pretty clear on Friday night.

"Someone who hurts other people's property. And shoes or something like that. I got a call from Tommy's mother. Apparently his sneakers melted."

"Melted?"

"That's what she said."

"How could that be someone else's fault other than Tommy's?" I pictured Marvin. In a cage.

"Other things melted too," she said.

"Melted?"

"That's the word the police kept using."

"The *police* said that someone melted Tommy's shoes? Why were you talking to police?" I pictured Marvin in the back of a police car. In jail. On trial.

Mom exhaled and blew her cheeks out. "Tommy told his mother that he thought you were the vandal."

"Tommy wanted to blow up the bulldozers once," I said. "If anybody's a vandal, it's him." Maybe because I ruined their fort, they decided to blame me for everything.

"I told them that you're a nice boy who cleans up other people's trash and that you hadn't hurt a thing in your life. Tommy's mother apologized for accusing you. She felt horrible."

"Huh."

She said, "I don't know what happened to that kid, but he's not the boy I used to know."

"Yeah," I said. "Me neither."

CHAPTER 29

ONE HUNDRED YEARS AGO

One hundred years ago, the Mexican Revolution was happening but not many people heard about it, even though by the time it was over, more than one million people died. One hundred years ago, my great-grandfather's tomato crop was dying of mold. His youngest daughter was dying of a disease no one could name and no one could cure. His *problem* was bigger than things that fit into a glass at Hannah's Bar or fit into the pockets of his wife's apron. His *problem* was making his liver sick. Making his skin sick. Making his whole body tired—so tired he couldn't work any-more. His *problem* was the bank man who came to visit the farm one day in September, right when a circus elephant named Mary was hanged in Tennessee for killing a trainer. His *problem* was bigger than that elephant. He hadn't paid his mortgage, and he would lose more than half the acreage of the farm.

The bank took *Phase One* and sold it in a sheriff's sale. One hundred years ago, another farmer was happy to buy one hundred acres of good soil for two thousand dollars. It was a steal.

CHAPTER 30

DOCTORS & DENS

There was melting. Melting wood, melting shoes, melting lino-
leum kitchen floors. There were accusations and guesses. Boys
blaming boys. Parents blaming parents.

One hundred years ago, no animal's scat melted anything,
anywhere.

One hundred years ago, no one would have believed the things
Ms. G taught our class about pollution. Some people still chose
not to believe in any of it while some people believed so much
they would do anything to make it all stop.

One hundred years ago, no one would have imagined that
humans would dump fourteen billion pounds of garbage into the
ocean every single year. One hundred years ago, no one would
have guessed that there could be a lake anywhere on Earth so

polluted with radioactivity that standing near it for five minutes could kill you dead.

Everything changes.

• • •

My nosebleed finally stopped at one o'clock. Mom told me to stay lying down and she brought me lunch on a tray like you get at a fast-food place. I didn't know where she got the tray; I'd never seen it before.

"We have a doctor's appointment for tomorrow," she said. She sounded annoyed.

"For my nose?"

"Yes."

I didn't think about what the nurse said about the smell of burning flesh. I didn't think about anything but how much I wanted to go outside and find Marvin's house and check on the scat circles. *What if Marvin's scat just kept eating all the way through everything? What if it never stopped and Marvin could make the whole world disappear?* I knew these were dumb kid thoughts. I was sure Marvin's scat wasn't going to melt the world. But I had to figure out just how bad it was. It was my job. Marvin was my friend.

"Mom, can I ask you a question?"

"Sure."

"What would you do if . . . I mean how would you handle a . . ." I lay there for a few minutes trying to figure out how to tell her, but I knew I couldn't. She was already annoyed with me about my nose.

"Is everything okay, Obe?"

"Forget it. I'm just a little scared of the doctor putting something up my nose," I lied.

"The receptionist said it's an easy procedure. Should only take a few minutes."

"Okay," I said.

At two o'clock, I said I wanted to take a walk. Mom said I had to stay on the couch, horizontal.

"But I've been getting nosebleeds for six months. You never made me lay on the couch this long before. It's boring."

"This was a bad one. Tomorrow we'll go get it fixed. I want you to stay put until then."

"I can't take a walk?"

I let that question hang in her ears for a while. I said it with just the right amount of pity and desperation mixed together. She was busy working on something on her computer.

She said, "Okay. But take a bunch of tissues with you. And don't wear your good sneakers."

•••

I knew where to go. I could get there before the bus brought Tommy and his friends home. I could avoid the workmen in *Phase Three* and Doug, the pickup-truck guy.

I walked past the creek, and then I jumped off the bank onto the shoulder of the road. I got to the sloped path to the river and walked to the riverbank that way. I knew Marvin's den, or what I thought was Marvin's den, was about seventy-five yards away.

The river was calm. It hadn't rained for a week, and that April was one of our driest. The river was still big, though. The Schuylkill River is wide, and when I looked at it from the bank, it was wider than I'd ever realized when looking at it from the bridge. There wasn't a path on the bank after a while, but there was still enough room for me to walk, and when it got a little scary, I could reach out and hold on to trees alongside the bank. As I neared where I thought Marvin's den was, there was brush piled up on the small path. In front of that was the roll of anti-erosion fencing. I heard splashing and the talking-clicking sound that Marvin made sometimes.

He saw me and let out a yelp and splashed. He was swimming in the deep water. Marvin was a good swimmer. I hadn't expected this. He swam like a Labrador retriever, but his legs were too short for that to be possible. How did he swim with half-hooves?

I watched him from the bank while he swam out into the middle of the river and did somersaults in the water. I kept watching until he came to shore and shook off the water like a dog and then disappeared into what must've been his den. He poked his head out. He smelled the air. He gave me a nod like he knew I was sitting right there, but he still just went into his den and didn't come out to say hello.

I didn't understand this. I thought we were friends. I called out, "Hey Marvin!" and when he didn't come out, I reckoned this was his way of inviting me into his house. I made my way down the steep bank until I was standing right next to it.

It was a hole. A den. A burrow, I guess. He was standing in its small doorway and was smiling that dumb grin he had. He sniffed the air again and walked to the fluorescent orange roll of anti-erosion fencing, ripped off a bite, and then went back to the den. He disappeared inside for a few seconds and then came out again.

His ears went up. Mine did too. Tommy and his friends were playing in the woods. Not near the fort. They were closer than that. They were moving. I could hear the brush being disturbed up at the top of the steep riverbank. I remembered the melting sneakers and the melting floors and I didn't want them to see the fencing or find Marvin's house.

I said, "Marvin, we have to get rid of that fencing."

He grinned at me.

I said, "We should push it in the water. It's bright orange. People will see it."

He made the talking noise. Clicking and breathing through his nose. He moved his front right hoof in a way like he wanted to play.

"We can't play. They're looking for you."

Marvin stepped back into his den. I poked my head in after him, and that's when I saw them.

CHAPTER 31

BABIES & ENEMIES

There were babies. Marvin Gardens babies. They weren't tiny babies — they were munching on small pieces of anti-erosion fencing — but they weren't as slimy as Marvin was. They were kind of fuzzy and they didn't have the under-biting jaw yet. More dog than pig so far. Four of them.

"This is awesome!" I said to Marvin. I smiled wide and patted him on his side. Mrs. Marvin Gardens was tucked into the back of the den, so I couldn't see her very well, but she looked almost the same as Marvin. I knew I'd have to give her a name of her own, because everyone should have a name of their own.

I went back to looking at Marvin's babies. Their eyes were blue and they were each about as big as a loaf of bread. The whole family clicked and chattered to one another and I just sat there with my head blocking the entrance to the den.

"Wow, Marvin. I don't know what to say. Congratulations,"

Mrs. Marvin had that grin on her face the way Marvin did and I could tell they were very proud of their babies. Mrs. Marvin was gnawing off tiny pieces of the anti-erosion fencing and the babies made sucking sounds as they ate it. They had teeth, but they were little teeth, like my old baby teeth.

I thought of the pollution solution, now increased by five. There had to be others. Animals don't just evolve out of nowhere and find mates and make babies like that. Marvin's kind must have been around for a while. Except nobody knew about them.

"How did you hide out for so long? Why doesn't anyone know about you?"

I was so happy Marvin existed and had a family. This was like being personal friends with the Loch Ness Monster or something. And then I remembered the rumors on the bus and the melting kitchen floors and shoes and realized that the babies also made the problem bigger.

More Marvins equaled more toxic scat. More Marvins meant more Marvins to protect. More Marvins meant the risk of a Marvin being shot by someone had just increased by five.

One of the babies made a noise and Marvin nudged it, to make it feel safe, I guess. I don't know how Marvin felt safe at all. Maybe he had no idea that his poop was eating holes in people's decks and kitchen floors. I could still hear the boys up at the edge of the woods.

I said, "Marvin, we're in trouble."

He grinned.

I said, "This is no time to smile."

He grinned wider.

I said, "I don't know how to save you."

He burrowed into his den and brought me the tennis ball. I knew I couldn't throw it — not even into the river — because if someone was looking for him, they'd see that from up on top of the bank.

I said, "We can't play. We have to be quiet." I held up a finger to my lips and said, "Shhhh."

Marvin understood this command. He dropped the tennis ball back into his den and lay down half in and half out of the den, with his head in my lap.

We sat there until we couldn't hear the boys anymore. I petted each one of Marvin's babies. The den smelled a little like Marvin's scat, but a lot calmer. The smell of the babies' tiny, bright orange baby poops wasn't nearly as bad as a full-grown Marvin scat.

As I sat there scratching Marvin's head, I wished this story didn't have to be about scat at all. There was so much at stake. So much to remember about this land and how it was being polluted with people. There was so much serious stuff to think about, and now it was coming down to poop.

"I have to go and look into something," I said. I patted Marvin's head and stood up, and he clicked at me until I was out of sight. I thought about kicking the anti-erosion fencing into the river, but the babies were eating it, and I knew that if I did that, I'd be polluting my own river.

Tommy and the boys were gone. That's what I hoped, anyway. I had to go to Marvin's bathroom and check the scat circles and see how big they'd grown. I had to know if Marvin's scat was going to melt the whole world.

So much had happened, I forgot about Annie until I saw her sitting by the creek.

CHAPTER 32

RIVERS & BLACK BEARS

There are babies!" I told Annie. "A mate and four babies. I found their den!"

She got up from the creek bank and said, "Really? Let's go!"

"I have to check something first. Remember when I told you I had more to tell you? I have to tell you that."

Annie frowned because I was frowning. She followed me as we walked to the woods, and I told her all about Marvin's scat—how I'd found it, how it dug pits in the soil, and how it might be a bigger problem than I'd thought.

"It smells horrible." she said. We weren't even to Marvin's bathroom yet. My nose had gotten used to it, maybe.

"Maybe it will melt the whole world."

Annie laughed at that. She said, "I don't think anything can melt the whole world. I mean, look at atomic bombs and stuff

155

like that. If the world lived through those, then the world can live with a little poop."

"It melted those kids' sneakers. And their floors!"

"So it's a weird kind of crazy poop or something. It can't melt rock. Rock is older than all of us," she said. "Look at this one. Just found it in the creek. Half a billion years old. Half a *billion*!"

When we got to the pits, they had grown to nearly double. I mean, wow. The scat had been Frisbee-sized. The pits, when I saw them last, were twice that width and six inches deep. Now, they were as wide as a Hula-Hoop and a foot deep, and the dead patches of grass were three feet in diameter. My measurement rocks were there, though, so that was good.

Annie said, "Ohhhh. So this is what melted the sneakers." I nodded. "I don't think you should worry about it," she said. "It's not hurting the rocks."

"Look at how deep they are!"

"It hasn't rained for a while. Maybe we could water them."

"I don't know," I said. I stood there and stared. Marvin's scat wasn't visible anymore. Maybe the pits would stop growing. I took a few rocks from around the area and put them on the perimeter of the biggest pit and looked at Annie.

She said, "Can we go down and see him now? I want to take pictures!"

I didn't know what to think of that. I wasn't sure I wanted Annie to be the one who took the first pictures of Marvin. I trusted her, but I wanted the pictures to myself the same as I'd wanted Marvin to myself before I told her about him.

"Let's go," I said. "We'll take the easy way." I walked her to the edge of *Phase Three* and we jogged on the road for about a minute until we found the path to the riverbank.

I could tell Annie was scared to be so close to the river. I understood it, because Annie wasn't just doing something dangerous. She was doing something dangerous while she was already breaking the rules. The river still seemed huge enough to eat us both and never tell anyone. That's what rivers do sometimes.

"Do you hear that?" I asked.

"The ticking noise?"

"It's Marvin talking. He knows we're here."

As we walked to Marvin's den, she kept her eyes on the path and didn't look out to the river anymore. We walked around the brush Marvin had built up on the path and then I showed Annie where to go. She got on her knees and leaned her head into the den.

"Hello!" she said. "Look at you all!" She was beaming.

"Aren't they cute?" I asked.

"So fuzzy. Not slimy yet like he is. And she's beautiful!" she said. She pulled her head out of the den's opening and looked at me. "Wow, Obe. This is really something, you know?"

I smiled. She smiled.

She said, "Have you named the rest of them yet?"

"Not yet. I just found them. Mrs. Marvin needs a special name."

She poked her head back into the den.

And then the worst thing happened.

Her phone rang.

It was a horrible ringtone that sounded like a dog barking. She pulled out of the den, startled. She hurled herself up onto the higher bank, sat down, and finally got the phone out of her zipped pocket. But she didn't answer it at first. It kept barking.

"It's my mom," she said.

Marvin started making a howling noise — same as the one he made the night he returned my flashlight but a little quieter. The barking ringtone was scaring him.

"Answer it!"

"But . . ." That's all Annie said to me. Her face said the rest. "Hello?" she said into the phone. Her face dropped even further. It was at sea level. I didn't hear what her mom was saying, but whatever it was, it wasn't good.

"I wasn't on a dangerous road," she said. Her mom said more stuff. "I'm . . . I'm down at Obe's house. I'm safe," she said. Her mom said more stuff. "I was going to come home before five," she said. Her mom said a lot more stuff until she hung up.

Annie said, "Crap. We have to get to your house in less than three minutes."

Marvin had stopped howling.

Annie had forgotten about taking pictures or naming Mrs. Marvin. She just rushed back down the path on the river-bank. I don't think she was even scared of the river anymore. I was. Moving that fast, one slip would put us into the water.

By the time we got over the creek and back to my house, Annie's mom's car was already in the driveway. My mom was out talking to her mom. We stopped at the edge of the wild patch and both of us took a deep, deep breath.

"I'm sorry," I said. I wasn't sure what I was sorry for.

"Don't be. I should be allowed out of my own yard, Obe. You showed me that."

"You're fearless, daring, and brave, Annie Bell."

She looked at me funny at first and then smiled. We walked to our respective mothers and Annie's mom didn't smile.

"You said you were at Obe's house. Where were you really?"

I looked at Mom and she didn't smile either. "We were at the creek," I said.

"It's really beautiful," Annie said. "Look at the rocks I got!" She pulled a few rocks from her pocket. Her mom still didn't smile.

"Obe spends a lot of time at the creek," Mom said.

"Annie knows the rules," Annie's mom said. "The rules do not include going to a creek with a boy."

"Obe isn't a boy!" Annie stuttered. "I mean, he's a boy, but he's my friend."

Annie's mom looked right in my eyes. "Friends don't take friends places that are dangerous."

I said, "The creek isn't dangerous. It's not even that deep. I'll show you if you want."

By this time, Annie's mom had said a few words to Mom in that low-mom tone and turned toward her car.

"See you later, Annie," I said.

"Bye. Thanks for today. It was fun," she said, glaring at her mother. Her mom looked back at me and gave me a look only my mom should be allowed to give me.

I didn't get it. Her mom liked me just fine the weekend before. I ate snickerdoodles and we played. What was so dangerous about leaving your own yard?

Mom and I went inside.

"You guys really were by the creek, right?" Mom asked. She motioned for me to sit on the sofa.

"Yeah. Annie collects rocks. But they don't let her out of her yard."

"Not at all?"

"No. I mean, they go places together and stuff, but Annie isn't allowed to go anywhere." Mom stayed quiet. "How is she supposed to find cool rocks in her own backyard?"

"I guess she could dig," Mom said.

"That's not the point!"

Mom put on her very serious face. "Listen, Obe. I need to talk to you about going out to the creek for the next few weeks. There's something dangerous going on. The police are looking into it, but for now we need you to stay closer to home."

"Something dangerous? Was that guy in the pickup truck a murderer or something?"

"What guy?"

"I saw him twice. He said he was looking for kids with paintballs or something. Said they were hurting the houses or bulldozers."

"You talked to him?"

"Yeah. He said he worked at the construction site. I don't know. He told me to keep my eyes open for anyone roaming around Phase Three."

She shook her head. "You know not to talk to strange people."

"He even told me his name was Doug. I don't think a guy who wanted to hurt me would tell me his name," I said.

She sat there thoughtful for a while. I moved to get up but she told me to stay sitting.

"The police think there's someone vandalizing the new development. First the melting sneakers and now this strange man, *and* there's an animal. They think it might be a black bear," she said. "I don't want you near the creek for a while."

Adults sure knew how to make up wild stories. I wanted to tell her that the animal wasn't a bear. I wanted to walk her down to the river and show her Marvin and his family. She'd have to believe it if she saw it, but I could tell she wasn't in the mood to believe anything.

"So I have to stay in the backyard too?" I asked.

"For now."

"I don't think the Doug guy is dangerous. He seemed nice. And I don't think there's a black bear. I'd have seen tracks."

"And you're sure you don't know anything about who's hurting people's property?" she asked.

"I'm sure."

She sighed. "There's a meeting tonight at the fire company. Some of the families around here want the game warden to come in and find the bear. Other families want the police to arrest whoever is doing stuff to their houses. I don't know. I was think-ing about going, but your dad says I should stay away." She looked kind of sad when she said that. The fire company was just across the river. It was built on Devlin land back in the 1970s. She'd always joked that it was the Devlin fire company.

"I'll go with you."

"It's for adults."

"Well, you're the only adult Devlin around, so I think you should go. None of this would be happening if they didn't come and wreck the field in the first place," I said. "And anyway, Dad can't tell you what to do."

Mom's cell phone rang and she answered it and handed it to me. It was Annie.

"I can't come over anymore. And I'm sorry if I got you in trouble."

"I'm sorry too," I said. "I hope you like the rocks you got from the creek," I said. One hundred years ago, people talked in code all the time.

"I love the rocks. I can't wait to get more. See you on Monday."

"Seat twelve," I said.

I handed the phone back to Mom. She listened to see if Annie's mom was going to come on the line, but then she hung up when no one was there.

"Do you have homework?" she asked.

For once, I didn't lie about math homework. Everything was too serious. "A math work sheet, reading, and some science stuff."

162

"I'm going to make some calls," she said. "You go do that in your room, okay?"

I said okay and took my backpack to my room, but once I got there, I didn't do homework. I worried. About everything. Because I knew there was no black bear. I knew there was no vandal. And if they were bringing in the game warden and the police, I knew I had to tell someone else about Marvin as soon as possible, because if I didn't, Marvin would end up dead. I ran through a list of possible adults I could tell. Mom and Dad were out because they were Mom and Dad and even though as parents go they were okay, I didn't want to drag them into this mess.

Annie's parents were out. Tommy's parents were out.

The only person I could think of to tell was Ms. G.

But I needed proof.

CHAPTER 33

SISTERS & RUMORS

There were sisters. Some were better than others. Tommy's older sister was pure mean and there wasn't anything he could do about it because nothing would fix her.

But I had Bernadette. She wouldn't believe me about Marvin because even though she was cool, I was still her little brother. But if I wanted to take pictures, I needed her camera phone, because my dumb plastic-encased unbreakable kid camera that I got when I was seven didn't take good pictures. We didn't have another camera in the house because Mom and Dad had camera phones too.

Dinner was weird. Mom talked the whole time about me getting my nose cauterized the next day, as if I was going to Disney World or somewhere interesting. Paris. Mexico. Nose cauterization.

"I'm so excited!" she said.

Dad just ate. He'd had a bad day at the store. So bad, he didn't even complain about it.

Bernadette just ate too. I didn't know what made her quiet, but I hoped she wasn't in a bad mood.

"You must be so relieved!" Mom said to me.

"I guess."

"I'd have done it sooner but I thought they would just go away," she said.

"What time's the appointment?" I asked.

"Ten. We'll just take you into school late."

Dad said, "Couldn't you get one after school?"

"It's sixth grade. What could he miss that's that important?" Mom answered.

A quiet came over the dinner table.

"Tommy's sister says you did something to her house," Bernadette said. "She said you melted the steps on her porch or something."

"I haven't been to Tommy's house since before Thanksgiving," I said.

"She told everyone on the team that you're a little jerk."

Mom said, "That girl was never anything but mean."

"She's a senior, so now she has the seniors hating on me."

"Girls," my dad said. He rolled his eyes and shook his head. It made Mom and Bernadette go back to eating their dinner.

Mom eventually said, "I'm sure the seniors don't hate you. And anyway, Obe didn't do anything to anyone's house."

"Sorry, Obe," Bernadette said.

"They're saying it to me on the bus too," I said. "When they figure it out, they'll stop."

"Figure what out?" she asked.

"Who put the holes in their stuff."

"You mean someone really did, like, go around putting holes in things?" Bernadette asked.

"That's what they say," Mom said.

I have no doubt people passed around rumors one hundred years ago. What else was there to do? One hundred years ago, I wondered, did someone pass a rumor around about my great-grandfather? I wondered if the people at Hannah's Bar knew he was about to lose all his land.

After dinner, I said I had to finish my homework. Mom said, "Clean your room while you're up there!" as if that was something I could just magically do.

I knocked on Bernadette's door and she told me to come in.

She was staring at her phone and looked frazzled, and when I asked why she said, "This stupid rumor won't die. What did you do?"

"I didn't do anything, I promise."

"Tommy's sister says you started some war or something."

"Started it?" I said. "Started it?" I got so mad, my face felt hot and I started to sweat and my hands rolled themselves into fists. "I didn't start *anything*."

"Your nose is bleeding," she said.

I got a few tissues and held them to my nose. "Do you know how I got these? Tommy sucker punched me in the nose after *he* started this stupid turf war."

"I will never understand boys."

"It wasn't me. That's the point. I wouldn't start a war. It's stupid. It's all *our* turf. It's our land."

She shook her head like she was disappointed in me.

"Anyway, I didn't melt holes in anything and this is all because of — um — something I want to talk to you about. Can you stop caring about the dumb seniors on the team and just put down your phone and help me?"

She put down her phone.

I said, "First, you have to promise me you won't tell anyone what I'm about to tell you." She held up her hand in a Scout's honor pose but she was giggling. "I'm serious," I said. "This is really serious."

"Okay," she said.

"Promise."

"I promise," she said. "Unless I have to tell, because if kids are beating you up at school or something, I have to tell."

"It's not about school."

"So?"

"I need to borrow your phone so I can take pictures of something tomorrow."

She stared at me. And then some more. "That's it?"

"No. You were supposed to say, 'Pictures of what?' " I said.

"Pictures of what?"

"I found an animal," I said. "I need a camera to take pictures of it because my camera is lame and the pictures are so small and blurry all the time."

"You found an animal." She didn't ask this. She just said it as if I found a rabbit or a snake or something. *Animals are Obe's groove, man.*

"I found a *new* animal. A totally new animal that's, like, the discovery of the century. Literally." I wasn't even exaggerating. One hundred years from now, an animal that solved the pollution problem would be the discovery of a century. If he didn't make it worse.

"I'm not giving you my phone," Bernadette said.

"I don't need the phone. I need the camera."

"Yeah. I'm not giving you that either."

I stood there with my hand to my nose with the tissues in place and I looked at her sideways. "I thought we were buds," I said. "I'd only need it from when you get home tomorrow to when I come back from the river."

"The animal is in the river?" She giggled a little again.

"Forget it. Just forget I ever said anything," I said. I wasn't stupid. Bernadette was mad at me for something I didn't even do. Her senior friends weren't talking to her and now there I was, telling her about Marvin Gardens, and she wasn't going to believe me.

"What's so special about the animal?" she asked.

"Seriously," I said, turning toward the door, "forget it. I shouldn't have even mentioned it."

I went back to my room and checked the tissues and my nose-bleed was pretty bad so I lay down and thought about the meeting tonight and how all those people would soon be in *Phase Three* and in the wild patch and the creek and the woods. They wouldn't know where Marvin's bathroom was. They'd walk through his scat and melt their own sneakers and get angrier and angrier until finally they'd find Marvin and do who-knows-what to him.

Maybe Marvin would know he was in danger and move his whole family down the river a few miles. It was probably how he got here in the first place. Maybe there was an entire population of Marvins upriver. Who knew?

Bernadette knocked on my door.

"Okay. You can take my phone," she said, "but you have to take me with you."

CHAPTER 34

BURNING FLESH & MS. G

There was the smell of burning flesh. The first nostril didn't hurt that much because the doctor numbed my nose first, but the smell was awful. The second nostril was harder. I couldn't sit still. Everything smelled like sulfur. I wiggled around while Mom tried to hold my head still so the doctor could get her hand near my face again. She looked into that nostril with her scope.

The doctor said, "We're going to have to use a different method on this side." She pulled out something that looked like a hot pair of tweezers. "You won't feel any pain," she said. "I numbed it."

It didn't matter what she said. I knew this one was going to hurt. She was going to burn my vein closed. In my nose. It took my mom yelling at me to get me to stop freaking out. "Obe! Sit still now! Right now!"

Mom didn't yell — ever. I sat still. It hurt. I felt the heat in my face and in my bones and the smell was something I wouldn't be able to shake. And my nose bled right then. A real gusher. No one told me *that* would happen.

The doctor said I was brave and gave me a Popsicle, which was hard to eat because of the tissues around both my nostrils.

"The bleeding should stop in five or ten minutes," the doctor said.

"Good," Mom said. "You'll make it to school today!"

"Don't blow your nose too hard or do too much exercise or heavy lifting for about a week, okay?" the doctor said.

"I'll make sure he doesn't. Thank you so much!" Mom said.

They were so cheery.

I just tried to eat the Popsicle.

On the way to school I asked Mom what the meeting was like the night before.

"Oh, it was nothing to write home about," she said. "Some hunters want to go and find the bear. Some other people want to find the vandals. They argued over whether the bear could be the vandal. The developer was there and said someone has been shooting his houses with some sort of paint."

"Paintballs. That's what that guy Doug told me."

"Anyway, people will figure out who to call about the bear. All of us agreed to keep you kids in sight until it's caught or . . . whatever they'll do with it."

I thought about the pictures I'd seen of bear traps. I didn't want Marvin getting caught in one of those. Even though I didn't have the pictures yet, I knew today was the day to tell Ms. G about Marvin. I hoped she wouldn't think I was exaggerating or lying.

I got to school in time for lunch. Right before science class, I found Tommy and Ms. G talking low by her desk. Instead of sitting down, I walked right over to them and said, "Stop telling people I melted your dumb sneakers. I didn't do anything."

Ms. G said, "Please sit down. Tommy and I were discussing something confidential."

I glared at him. He didn't wink. He didn't smile. He didn't even seem like he was telling her about Marvin Gardens. He looked in trouble.

"Sorry," I said.

"Are you okay?" she asked.

"I was at the doctor this morning," I said. "I'm a little weird today, I guess."

I sat down. The rest of the class filtered in and Tommy skulked away from Ms. G's desk and sat down in his seat. I didn't know what I'd missed the day before, but it looked to me like Tommy had gone overboard like he did sometimes. You just couldn't control him in that class on account of his crush on Ms. G.

She called me to her desk after Tommy sat down. "I have makeup homework for you from yesterday," she said. "And we watched a short documentary." She handed me a Post-it Note. "Here's the link so you can watch it at home."

"Thank you."

"You didn't miss too much. You'll see on my note what you have to read in the book to catch up."

"Okay," I said. I kept standing there and the class was getting quiet behind me. "Do you, um — have time after class to talk to me about something?" I asked.

"I have about five minutes, I guess. Otherwise, you can come to me at afternoon homeroom."

"Okay. I'll see you after class."

"Is everything all right?" she asked.

"I'm not sure. It's hard to explain. I need your help," I said.

I'd never said anything so perfect in my life. *I need your help* was the very best thing to say to Ms. G, because she was the kind of teacher who would actually help. She smiled and said, "I'll see you later."

We talked about air pollution in class. A human being breathes about twenty thousand liters of air every day. Kids are more susceptible to air pollution because we breathe more and our bodies are smaller. Back in the old days — 1952 — there was a thing called the Great Smog Disaster in London, England, and four thousand people died in less than a week from smog. Smog is a highly concentrated fog of pollution. These days, Beijing, China, has a smog concentration that's twelve times higher than the safe level and people walk around in masks. More than twenty-one million people live in Beijing. That's a lot of masks. But smog is everywhere, really. New Delhi, India. Los Angeles, California. Mexico City, Mexico. New York City. Even little towns could be affected by smog. Ms. G told us about Donora, Pennsylvania — only five hours west of us — where twenty people died and more than seven thousand got sick from smog in 1948. That smog was chemical smog — a factory released some bad stuff and the weather held it in the air. A lot of other smog disasters, like the one in London in 1952, were caused by burning coal.

The more I learned about pollution, the more humans looked dumb. I mean, if we knew we were poisoning the oceans, why didn't we stop? If people died because of smog, why didn't we stop filling the air with it? I was getting to the point in Earth Month where I wanted Earth Month to be over so I didn't have to feel frustrated and sad all the time.

After class, I felt like I was losing my nerve, but I knew I had to tell somebody about Marvin Gardens. Annie knew but she couldn't help from her backyard. Telling Bernadette wasn't enough because she was fourteen and wouldn't know what to do. I needed Ms. G. I went up to the front of the room.

"You're doing very well in my class, Obe," she said.

"That's good," I said.

"So what help do you need?"

"I have a secret," I said. She just looked at me. "I mean, I found something that I don't know what to do with."

She looked alarmed. She said, "Should I call the principal?"

"No!"

"Did you find it in school?"

"I should start over — I — I don't quite know how to explain this without looking crazy — like those people who say they saw Bigfoot."

"I believe in Bigfoot," she said. She smiled wide.

This changed everything.

I let out a big breath and just said it. "You know I live over by Devlin Creek, right? So two weeks ago I found this animal, and it's not like any other animal that ever lived before. It eats plastic. Only plastic. Like plastic bottles and yogurt containers and shopping bags and pretty much anything as long as it's plastic."

"Go on," she said.

"So I don't know what to do about it."

"What do you want to do?"

"Well, the other kids who live there now—you know my family's field got turned into a development. Those kids have seen it. Tommy, really. Tommy saw the animal and now he and his friends are trying to kill it."

"Kill it? Why would they want to kill it?"

I shrugged. "The adults had a meeting last night at the fire company. They think there's a bear on the loose. But it's not a bear. It's this animal. He's not dangerous, but there are hunters in the neighborhood who want to kill him too."

"Seems a bit rash," she said.

"Humans are scared of things. They don't like, you know, when a kid doesn't wear the right kind of sneakers. So they make fun of him."

Ms. G frowned and put her finger to her lips like she was figuring out a puzzle. She said, "Are you being bullied?"

"No. Not really."

"Not really?"

"I wanted to talk to you about the animal. You're a scientist. I'm just a kid. I don't know what to do about him. He really does eat plastic. Maybe he could be the solution or something. To the pollution problem."

"He?"

"The animal is a he. You know." I blushed then.

"He lives in your creek?"

"He wanders up there, but he lives somewhere else," I said. "I found his den yesterday. I know more, but I don't want to tell anybody in case I get in trouble. I couldn't tell my parents about the animal because I didn't think they'd believe me. But if you believe in Bigfoot, then you might be able to help us."

"Why would you get in trouble?" she asked.

"So, what do I do?" I said. "Do I call somebody — like a game warden or something? I looked them up on the Internet and mostly it says they sell hunting licenses."

"I don't know," Ms. G said. "I'm going to have to think about it."

Kids started to come into the classroom. "I'm going to get a picture of him tonight. I'm taking my sister down to meet him. Just don't tell anybody, okay?"

"I won't tell anyone," she said. "And if you want to talk more about kids being mean to other kids, you know you can come to me, right?"

"It's really not about that," I said.

"It's about the animal," she said. "I know."

CHAPTER 35

PAINTBALLS & PICTURES

There were ridiculous things that people said.

Annie Bell said to me on the bus, "They told me that if I sat too close to you, you'd melt my eyeballs out."

"They're stupid."

"I know," she said. "Just thought you'd want to know that you're now an eyeball melter." We both laughed.

"So, did you get in big trouble? From yesterday?"

"Not big trouble. I'm just supposed to stay in the yard again now."

"Me too. They think there's a bear," I said.

"I know. I heard about the meeting." She rolled her eyes. "They're so dramatic."

Annie pulled out a spiral-bound notebook from her backpack. She turned to a page where she'd drawn Marvin Gardens. It was better than every drawing I'd tried to make.

"Dude! You're good!" I said.

She leafed through a lot of pages where there were failed drawings. "It took me a while to get it right."

"I've been trying for two weeks and I haven't done anything that good at all. Tonight Bernadette and I are going down to take some pictures of him. Maybe I can draw him better then."

She scowled. "I wanted to get the first pictures."

"I know. I don't even know how we'll get down there. My mom has us all on watch."

"Just show me the pictures if you get them, okay?"

I nodded.

"Oh, and I thought of something," Annie said. She smiled. "Boardwalk."

I had no idea what she was talking about. My face must have shown this.

"Mrs. Marvin's name. Boardwalk. What do you think?"

It was perfect. Not just the name, but Annie's grasp of irony. My first response was to say *I love you* to Annie. Not because I wanted to marry her or anything, but because she was like the little sister I never had or the best friend I always wanted. And because she came up with the name Boardwalk. But boys can't go around saying *I love you* to other kids. Kind of sad if you ask me, but then again, I was the hippie. So I said, "I think it's just perfect."

•••

Mom greeted me with "You still haven't been handing in your math homework."

That wasn't quite right. I hadn't been *doing* my math homework, so of course I wasn't handing it in. The last time I saw it was at the bottom of my backpack, imitating the bellows of an accordion.

"I'll get caught up," I said.

"You'll sit here and get caught up right now," she said. "Dad's working until closing, so it's just the three of us for dinner."

Bernadette wouldn't be home for another two hours because of softball, so I sat down and smoothed out the two math work sheets and stared at them.

Something was different about Mom. She was never mad. She could be disappointed or sometimes sad and she looked tired a lot, but she was never mad.

"Are you mad at me?"

"A little."

"Are you mad at something else?"

She sighed and sat down next to me at the kitchen table. I thought she was going to say something about the black bear or the melting stuff. Instead she said, "I want you to do well in school. I want you to go to a good college and get a good job. Your father and I didn't have the opportunity to do that, you know? We want both of you to succeed."

"Yeah. Okay," I said.

Mom was quiet for a while. Then she said, "They reduced my hours today. At work. Again."

"Aw, that stinks, Mom," I said.

"I have to look for a new job, and what do I have? I don't have a big list of degrees or education on my resume. I don't have any skills, really, outside the jobs I already worked. Today of all days I want you to do better at school. I want you to understand, even though you're only in sixth grade, that this stuff actually *matters*."

"I know. I really know it matters. I promise."

"Good." She reached over and patted my hand, and something in the way she looked at me told me she hadn't told Dad yet. I knew why. Dad probably *blah blah blahed* to her about stuff too. No offense to him, but he had a knack for making things worse.

"After I finish this, I'll get started on my science project. That way I'll be ahead." This was true. My science project involved me and Bernadette walking down to the river . . . now made more difficult by the fact that we weren't allowed to leave our backyard.

"Good boy," she said.

•••

Bernadette wasn't in her bad mood anymore when she got home.

"I'm starting in tomorrow's game," she said. "*Starting*." Starting was a big deal. It was one thing to be a varsity freshman, but a *starting varsity freshman*? That was huge.

"That's awesome," I said.

"So are we taking that walk?" she asked.

"I told Mom it's my science project. And it kind of is, I guess." She pulled her phone from her pocket and said, "Let's do it!"

She went to call up to Mom, who was in her bedroom, but I stopped her. "You can't tell her. She thinks there's a bear down by the river. There was a meeting last night."

"I heard about the meeting."

"Let's just sneak down and get back as soon as we can," I said.

"But there's no bear, right?"

"No bear," I said. "Promise."

As we walked Gilbrand Road down the hill, it was crowded with rush-hour traffic, so I climbed up the bank into the dirt lots of *Phase Three*. Bernadette followed me. We walked on the edge of the bank until we got to the railroad tracks and I told her we had to go back to the road until we came to the path to the river.

"Let me lead," I said. "You just stay ready with the camera."

She let me lead and she kept saying these weird things like "The river is really beautiful" and "I should come down here more often." Bernadette had always left the creek to me and Tommy. Even when we were little, she'd rather listen to her 1960s music and try to dance like they did back then—like she was imitating a tree in wind or the ocean or something.

As we got closer to the river, it smelled like river and a little bit like Marvin's scat. Bernadette said, "I take it back. It smells gross down here."

The anti-erosion fencing was gone. Once I saw the brush blocking the path, I knew to walk up into the trees on the bank, and Bernadette followed me. I said, "Promise not to freak out when you see him, okay?"

"Okay. It's not, like, Bigfoot or something, right?"

"He's small. Like a dog."

I called out to Marvin and heard the talking noise he made. I was so relieved he was there. Bernadette and her camera were ready. I motioned for her to stay behind the den, and I went around to the other side. Marvin was in the doorway, but he wasn't himself.

He had paint on his slimy skin. The splotch looked like someone had thrown paint at him — not like he'd been rolling in it or anything like that. It was blue. I got a feeling of panic like on the day Tommy sucker punched me. "How'd you get that paint all over you, Marvin? Are you okay?"

"Marvin?" Bernadette asked.

Marvin stuck his snout in the air and sniffed. I said, "I brought my sister to meet you. Come out and say hello."

He walked slowly out of the den and poked his head around to look at Bernadette. He wasn't moving right. He didn't have the right balance or something.

She just stood there.

"Pictures!" I whispered.

She stared at him.

"Come on! Give me the camera!"

She handed me the phone, and as Marvin walked slowly to meet her, I took as many pictures as I could. I could only see his blue side, so I moved up onto the bank. He didn't have any paint on his other side, so I took more pictures.

Bernadette said, "What is he?"

"I don't know."

"Why is he blue?"

"It's paint. He didn't have it on him yesterday."

He still wasn't walking right. He was limping. Marvin burped. It smelled like sewage.

Bernadette said, "That's disgusting."

"He eats plastic."

"No, he doesn't," she said.

"I'm serious. That's how I met him. Eating a plastic water bottle. And then a shopping bag. He eats any kind of plastic, really." I kept taking pictures of Marvin as he sniffed around Bernadette's shoes. He was moving a little faster now.

"He's slimy!" she said.

"Yeah. He's got skin like algae."

"Weird."

Marvin made the talking sound and I reached down and patted his head.

"He's kind of ugly looking," Bernadette whispered.

"He's just different," I said. I turned to Marvin. "What happened to the fencing, buddy? Did you get rid of it like I told you?"

"Does he understand English?" Bernadette asked.

"No."

"So why are you talking to him like he does?"

"He's my friend."

"I worry about you."

"I want to get pictures of the rest of the family," I said, and I moved toward the den. Bernadette stayed where she was.

I took about eighty pictures in all and I had time to scroll through them and make sure at least one of them would work for Ms. G when I talked to her about Marvin the next day. Some were blurry. The den was dark but I didn't want to turn on the flash and freak out Boardwalk or the babies.

While I was in the den, Marvin found a plastic cup to munch on. *CREWAHARKKKLTKELTH!* Bernadette watched him eat the cup with her hands over her ears and looked genuinely frightened, so I smiled at her and she gave me a pained smile in return.

"Mom's going to ring the dinner bell soon," I said.

"So we just leave him here?"

"This is where he lives."

"But I thought you wanted to save him or something. Man, what's that smell? It's so rank," she said.

"I'll tell you on the way home," I said. I snapped a few pictures of Marvin eating the cup. The blue paint on his side looked painful. "Does that look like somebody shot him with a paintball?"

"The back of the stop signs all over the developments have the same marks, don't they? I know some of the girls on the team have boyfriends who do that kind of stuff. They go out in the woods and shoot each other with paintball guns and pretend to play war."

"Oh," I said. "Now I get what a paintball is." I turned to Marvin. "Buddy, who shot you?" I looked back at Bernadette. "He's usually a lot more energetic," I said.

As if he could understand what I was saying, Marvin let out a small whimper. He was breathing heavily.

"I'll be back tomorrow," I said to him. "Stay, okay? Just stay."

"He's trained?" Bernadette asked.

"A little. Let's go before Mom finds out we left. She's having a bad day as it is."

"She is?"

I said, "I'll explain when we get back up the hill."

Bernadette led the way to the road. She still had on her sweat-pants and cleats. I told her to watch out for anything that looked like poop, and not to step in it.

By the time we climbed up the bank into *Phase Three*, I was out of breath and I thought I was going to get a nosebleed, but I didn't get one. It felt like a personal victory.

CHAPTER 36

CLEARING HISTORY & THE CLOUD

There were details. I didn't know them. I told Bernadette about Mom's work cutting her hours and how she'd lectured me on going to college.

"Get used to that lecture. She gives it, like, once a week once you hit high school," she said.

"She just wants what's best for us."

Bernadette said, "So that animal — he's — um — endangered?"

"He's undiscovered."

"He eats plastic," she said.

"He could save the world," I said.

She walked quietly for a few seconds and then she said, "Dude. You're going to be famous."

I shrugged this off.

"I'm serious. You're going to end up one of those genius scientists or something."

"I don't know," I said.

She went quiet again until she said, "I worry about you sometimes. You don't see how great you are. Tommy isn't the only friend in the world. He's not even a good friend. You're worth getting to know, Obe. You're smart and funny and you're sweet, you know?"

"I have Annie, and she's a good friend."

"Oh. Well, that's good. I'd like to meet her," she said. "Just so you know you're a good person. I know this has all been hard for you, and I know Mom and Dad don't help much. But we all just want you to be happy."

"I'm happy. But now I'm worried more than anything. Mostly about Marvin."

"I'm telling you. You're going to be famous. Just promise I can play myself in the movie they make about you one day, okay?"

We both laughed at that. On the inside, I felt better than I had in a long time. Up until that moment, I kind of thought Annie was my friend because she felt sorry for me. But now, I realized that maybe I'd been selling myself short. I wanted to hug Bernadette for being so nice, but she was walking too fast and she wasn't much of a hugger.

When we got in, Mom didn't know we'd been gone. She asked, "You weren't out near the creek, were you?" We said no, which wasn't a lie.

After dinner, Bernadette helped me upload the pictures of Marvin Gardens to the computer. She showed me how to post them to a private online folder and wrote down the address, password, and all that stuff as if I'd never used a computer before. While Mom did something in the garage, I went through each picture and enlarged the blue paint splotch on Marvin's side. I could see a raised lump there — like a bruise or sore where the paintball had hit him. How long would it take for him to get hit with a real bullet and not just paint?

I fixed the pictures of Boardwalk and the babies so they were lighter and saved them to the private folder. I wanted to write something about the whole experience — actually make this my science project. Marvin wasn't the perfect solution to plastic pollution yet. There was the matter of the scat. If I wrote a paper for my science project about Marvin and didn't include that information, I'd be a very bad scientist, and I didn't want to be a bad scientist because Ms. G didn't accept bad science.

"I want to see all your math homework before you go to bed!" Mom called from the door to the garage.

"Okay!"

"She's coming," Bernadette said. "Sign out of that window. Clear your history."

"What?"

"Clear your history!" she whispered. "On the computer."

I had no idea how to do this. Bernadette came to the computer and did it for me. "Now Mom can't see the websites you visited," she said.

"Wow. You're sneaky," I said.

I wanted to make sure I could sign back into the account with the private folder of pictures, so when Mom went out to the garage, I signed in, found the pictures, signed out again, and cleared my history.

I did the two sheets of math homework I'd left on the table, then I opened my science notebook and started writing down the story of how I found Marvin. I started with the first day but I didn't say anything about how I thought he was eating my liver. I got all the way to today, when I saw the welt on his side.

I wrote questions at the bottom.

Who can help me?

What will they do with Marvin if I take them to him?

Will he be able to stay with his family?

Will his toxic waste turn out to be worse for the environment than the plastic he eats?

That last question was a doozy.

It was still light outside and Dad wasn't due home for another two hours. Tommy and his friends would still be at baseball practice so I knew what I had to do.

"Can I borrow your phone to take some pictures of a few other things?" I asked Bernadette.

She thought about it for a minute. "Do NOT look at my texts," she said.

"I promise. I just need the camera."

She handed me the phone. I made sure Mom was still in the garage and I headed toward the creek. Marvin wasn't there, but

I didn't want him to be there. I wanted him to be safe with his family in his den. What *was* there, beyond my official turf line and closer to the woods, were the pits and the dead spots in his bathroom.

I tiptoed around the circles I'd marked. The oldest ones had stopped growing. They were still the size of a Hula-Hoop. I checked a few other circles and they weren't growing much more either. The earth wouldn't melt. This was a relief.

I went to the place on Orchard Way where I'd seen Marvin's multicolored scat on the road two Sundays before. Even though it had rained then, right through our Sunday dinner, the road had a small divot in it, and the gutter that led to the drain grate had a gully carved out of it too.

I took pictures of all of it and put Bernadette's phone in my pocket.

A car drove toward me on the road and I stepped onto the sidewalk and walked toward my house. The car slowed down. I tried not to look at who was in it. But then it slowed down more and drove alongside me and I finally looked over. It was Tommy's sister driving the car.

"Little jerk!" she yelled.

I walked faster.

"Hey, you little jerk! You better not mess with my house again!"

I ran. Instead of going the long way to my house, I cut between the two houses behind my house and into my backyard. A dog was barking, but I didn't care. All I could hear was Tommy's sister in my head. *You little jerk. You little jerk. You little jerk.*

I checked my pocket for Bernadette's phone and it was still there.

I stopped on the back porch to shake off all my feelings. I felt like crying. I felt like yelling. None of it made any sense.

Bernadette's phone made a noise like she got a text and I looked by instinct. The text was from Tommy's sister. It said *I'm making sure you get kicked off the team. Good riddance.*

I took a few deep breaths and then went inside to the computer. I wanted to connect Bernadette's phone to it the way she had before but I was afraid to mess her phone up so I went and got her. I wanted to erase Tommy's sister's text but I couldn't do it. Instead I handed her the phone and asked for her help and she came downstairs and helped me take the right pictures off the phone and put them in the private folder. I printed one picture for Annie because I thought she'd like to see it, and I folded it four times and stuffed it into the front pocket of my backpack.

I decided that the name *Private Folder* was too vague so I renamed it *Marvin Gardens*.

"Marvin Gardens?" Bernadette asked.

I answered, "It's ironic, right?" She nodded like she understood. I wanted to talk to her about the text from Tommy's sister but I didn't say a word.

"You're all set," she said. "The new pictures are on the cloud." She got up and scrolled on her phone to see the texts she missed. I watched her face, but it didn't change a bit.

One hundred years ago, my great grandfather would have never believed there would be texting and camera phones and computers and private folders on something called *the cloud*. One hundred years ago, my great-grandfather wouldn't have cared, I bet. He was too busy drinking dirt to care about much else but drinking more dirt.

I went to bed before Dad even got home from work. I didn't go to sleep right away. I wrote more in my science notebook about Marvin. I reported on the scat and what it was doing to the land.

I decided to turn off my light and try to sleep but I was too nervous about talking to Ms. G the next day. I had no choice. I'd already put everything into motion. And now I had pictures and a first draft of a project paper.

By the time Dad started *blah blah blahing* downstairs about Mom's boss, I'd given up going to sleep and just lay there with my head sandwiched between two pillows.

One hundred years ago, if an animal was ruining the land, it would be shot.

I was afraid, even though so many other things had changed in the world in one hundred years, that this wasn't one of them.

CHAPTER 37

ONE HUNDRED YEARS AGO

One hundred years ago or so, two cars drove up the driveway to my great-grandparents' farm. They may have been the first cars to ever drive up the driveway because in 1917 it was rare to see a car that far from town. There were four men in the car and they stepped out one by one, each of them in a suit and a long black overcoat. By the time they got out, my great-grandmother and her kids were all out on the back porch. I wonder what they must have been thinking, seeing these men get out of the car. Those kids never had but one pair of shoes.

The men in the coats talked to my great-grandmother and told her that the land was the bank's land now and they were there to take inventory of the farm equipment in the barn. She told them to go ahead and she made the children go back into the house. She stood and watched the men walk around like they owned the place. She didn't have a phone or any way to find out what she'd lost, but in her heart she knew she'd lost it all.

CHAPTER 38

PLANS & PROMISES

There wasn't time.

Annie wasn't at her bus stop but she was running toward it. By the time she got into seat twelve, she was out of breath. "Overslept," she said.

I reached into my backpack pocket and handed her the folded piece of paper. "You can have it," I said.

She opened it and we hunched over and looked at Marvin Gardens. It was one of my better shots, one of Marvin eating the cup. She said, "This is great!"

"I told Ms. G yesterday. She's going to help us."

"How?"

"I don't know, but since that meeting, I think we need help fast," I said.

"My dad said they're calling the game warden to set traps," she said.

As the bus got closer to school, my nerves went up. Annie must have seen it on my face. "Here," she said. She reached into her jeans pocket and pulled out a smooth, bluish slate rock. "I got it on the beach at a state park in Oregon. It'll bring you good luck."

•••

By the time I got off the bus and walked to Ms. G's room, there were two kids waiting for her help already. One of them was Tommy.

I didn't even walk through the doorway. Ms. G saw this and I saw her see it. I walked to my own morning homeroom and sat at my desk and stared into space. I swear I could have put my head down in my arms and fallen asleep right there.

The pollution fact of the day on the announcements was: *About 80 percent of the trash in our landfills could be recycled. Recycle when you can! It makes all the difference.*

I didn't hear a word of our social studies lesson. I think we talked about the Civil War. Gray and blue uniforms. I couldn't remember which was which. I didn't even look at the math homework that was handed back before I turned it into an accordion in the bottom of my backpack. And then the classroom phone rang and Mr. Mustache told me to report to Ms. G's room.

That woke me up.

She met me at her classroom door. "I have a free period and

I want to talk some more about what you told me yesterday," she said.

"I have a bunch of pictures and I wrote a report," I said.

"Pictures of what?"

"The animal. I just need a computer."

She looked impressed. "How about we go to the library?" she said.

As we walked to the library I asked, "Do you really believe in Bigfoot?"

"Yep."

"What about aliens? Or UFOs? Do you believe in them?"

She took a second to answer that one. "I'm not sure what I believe, but I hope there's more intelligent life out there, I guess."

We set ourselves up at a corner computer in the library. I put in the address and my password. I found my Marvin Gardens folder and looked over at Ms. G. "Are you ready?"

"Ready."

I opened the folder. I scrolled through the pictures, and she sat forward to get a good look. I said, "The blue paint wasn't there until yesterday. I think someone shot him with a paintball. They do it to the road signs around my house too."

"Wow." That's all she said as I scrolled.

When I got to the picture of Marvin eating the plastic cup, I said, "So I told you he eats plastic, right? Only plastic too. I've never seen him eat anything else."

"Is that your sister's foot?" she asked.

"Yeah."

"So he's about the size of a dog? Maybe a beagle?"

"Bigger than a beagle, but not by much," I answered.

"And those are babies? There's more than one?"

"Four babies, Marvin, that's what I named him, and his—um—mate. Six in all."

"I can't believe this, Obe."

"I know the feeling," I said.

"It's extraordinary!"

"He's pretty smart too. He fetches like a dog, sits, and stays pretty much."

"Is that the creek you're standing by?"

"The river. The Schuylkill River."

"This is fascinating. Just amazing."

"I still need your help."

She took a deep breath. "Now I understand." She took another deep breath. "I had no idea."

"There was a meeting. You know that, right? They think there's a black bear on the loose. And now someone shot Marvin with a paintball. I need to get his whole family out of there and move them somewhere safe."

"Weird feet."

"Half hoof and half paw. He swims pretty well too."

I scrolled more slowly as I got to the scat pictures. She was still sitting forward, her mouth slightly open, and I stopped to get my notebook.

"I wrote the history of finding him here," I said. "He's not all perfect, though."

She took the notebook and started reading.

"Sorry about my spelling and handwriting. I wrote it out fast last night."

"It's fine."

"I was thinking maybe I could make this my contest project. But I don't really know if it will work. I mean, if he moves on or if a game warden comes to take him away, then I can't really win a contest with an animal who doesn't live there anymore."

"This is the perfect contest project," she said. "You've discovered something really important."

She kept reading. She got to the second part—about the problem.

"Do you have pictures of the scat?" she asked.

I scrolled through all the pictures I'd taken.

"Hold on. Back up," she said. "It melted the road?"

"Yeah."

She leaned right up to the screen and enlarged the image. "But not the metal?"

I looked at the picture of the road. I'd been so distracted by Tommy's sister driving up behind me that day, I never noticed that the metal grate was fine. I mean I knew it was, but I didn't think anything of it.

"Seems not," I said.

"This is really extraordinary, Obe. It's exciting," she said. "Do you mind if I scroll through all of them again?"

After five minutes of scrolling, she said, "I think we should figure out a plan of action."

Finally. The relief I felt was ten times what I felt when I'd showed Annie and Bernadette. I knew Ms. G was going to come up with a plan—a real plan to make sure everything worked out. After all, this was a woman who collected a million soda can tabs.

She added, "Do your parents know about any of this?"

"No way."

"You said Tommy knows, right?"

"Tommy and his friends try to lure him onto their turf by putting plastic all over the woods."

"I didn't know people had *turf* anymore."

"Yeah. Me neither until Tommy and his friends won it from me."

She leaned her head. "How does one *win* turf?"

I really didn't want to get into this. "I really don't want to get into that," I said. "It's over. They won the turf. End of story."

She gave me the adult-eye. You know the one. One eye squints and the other one half-squints. "Was there any fighting involved in the winning of this turf?"

"Not really," I said. "It doesn't matter anymore anyway. We just have to save Marvin Gardens."

She smiled when I said his full name. She looked back at a few of the pictures. The one of the scat circles had *Phase Three* in the background.

"It must have been really sad for you," she said.

"What?"

"Losing that cornfield. Having all these new neighbors."

I didn't know what word really covered that feeling. Sad was too small. Devastating was too dramatic. I just nodded.

"My family used to get our apples from Mr. Willard's orchard. I know it was sad for us to see all those trees go. Couldn't have been easy for your family."

This is what made Ms. G a legend. She was a real human being. She'd saved Bernadette from her horrible math teacher year by actually caring — the same as this. It's what made me think I might one day want to be a teacher. Well, that and doing cool experiments that made kids care about science. Annie could be Dr. Annie Bell. I'd be fine with Mr. Obe Devlin if I could grow crystals, dissect frogs, and make vinegar and baking soda volcanoes a few times per year.

"So who do we call?" I asked. "The game warden? A scientist?"

"We start with the game warden. But I want a biologist there too. I have someone in mind."

"You?"

"I wish!" she said, and then laughed. "But I chose to be a teacher. I went to college with a woman who should be able to help us. I was just talking to her last week. You go back to class when the bell rings. I'll talk to her over my lunch. I'll have a plan by science class. We have to protect him fast."

"I want to be there. I mean, when the game warden sees him.

I don't know if Marvin will be mean to strangers or anything. I don't want him to be scared," I said.

"We'll make sure you're there."

"Promise?"

"Promise."

CHAPTER 39

FIERCE & READY

There were *problems.* Some were bigger than others. My nose-bleeds were gone, my secret was shared, and Marvin Gardens might be saved. But Tommy still wasn't my friend and sometimes that made me sadder than losing the field.

I saw Tommy at lunch, and I decided to sit at the table right next to him and his friends. I don't know what got into me, but I wasn't scared of any of them. Not in school. Maybe not out of school either. Something about having a secret as big as Marvin Gardens — something about having a *plan* with Ms. G made me feel safe.

The boys didn't say a word to me while I ate my lunch. Some other kids sat down at the table and said hello. Nice kids, but in their own group. They talked about video games.

I thought about Tommy and his *problem*. He wanted more friends, I guess. He wanted a bigger audience or a cooler life. He wanted to grow up. That's what he said to me once — that I shouldn't be playing in the creek like a kid anymore. But I was a kid. And he wanted to be a man or a teenager or something other than a kid. That was Tommy's *problem*. Luckily for him, you can't stop time. He would eventually solve his problem just by getting older.

Language Arts class — the one right before science — was the longest class I ever sat through. Verb tense discussions always reminded me of that joke Dad told about how past and present walk into a bar . . . and it's tense.

Old joke, but it still cracked me up.

One hundred years ago, tea bags, escalators, and instant coffee were all relatively new things. But past tense was still past and present tense was still present. It was good to know that some things didn't change. In fact, the idea of it made me calm and almost sleepy.

I yawned.

The bell rang.

I walked so fast to Ms. G's room, I was the first one there.

"Did you talk to your friend?" I asked.

"I did. Can you come during afternoon homeroom? I'll tell you more then. She's calling the game warden now and we'll all meet later today if that's okay. At your house."

"Meet at my house? Today?"

"The animal needs help. You said so in your report."

"He does," I said.

"Today it is, then. About four thirty?"

"I guess I should tell my parents."

"I guess you should."

I didn't get home right away to tell my parents, though. On the bus, I told Annie everything about what Ms. G said, and when her stop came, she ducked down so the bus driver wouldn't see her and didn't get off. I said, "What are you doing?"

"Shh."

"Your parents are going to freak out!" I whispered.

"Shh!"

The bus moved on. Annie stayed crouched beside me. I leaned down.

Annie said, "I want to see him again in case they take him away."

"I don't think they're going to take him away."

"I'm coming anyway."

I smiled. The bus stopped at my stop and Annie walked off like she belonged there and the bus driver didn't seem to notice. We went directly to the creek because neither of us were allowed there and if my mom saw Annie, she'd know we were up to something.

Annie dropped her backpack in the tall grass of the wild patch and started to walk toward the river. "I only have fifteen minutes," she said. "My dad gets home from work at four."

"Come on. Let's go see if we can find him."

We jogged through *Phase Three* and I stopped when I saw him over by the railroad tracks.

Annie pointed. Marvin saw me, but didn't run toward me. We'd have to cross the tracks to get to him. I said, "Wait up! Hold on! The tracks!"

She kept jogging and I jogged next to her.

"Be careful!" I said.

"Of what?"

"The tracks. The train!"

"Logically, if a train was coming, we'd hear it. More logically, we just have to look both ways before we cross. Right? Or is this a magical, invisible train?"

Talk about daring, fearless, and brave.

Marvin walked over and he was still a bit slow from the blue paint, but he seemed more like himself. He grinned.

"Hi Marvin!" Annie waved. Marvin's nubby tail wagged.

"Marvin, you remember my best friend, Annie, right?" I said.

Marvin came to us and lay down.

Annie said, "I didn't know I was your best friend."

"Well, yeah," I said.

She petted Marvin's head again, and she didn't even get grossed out by the slime. I gave Marvin a plastic bag that I had in my backpack. He slurped it into his mouth and purred as he ate it. Annie kept petting his head, behind his ears. "Poor guy. That's a paintball all right. Who would shoot an animal with a paintball?" Marvin sniffed her and moved his head like it felt nice and then he made that noise — the clicking.

"Shoot. We probably won't have time to see the whole family today." I pointed toward the river. This reminded me of telling

Mom about our visitors. "You have to leave now to get home before four," I said. "Ms. G is coming at four thirty with those people."

"One more minute." She kept petting his head.

"I have to go tell my parents that people are coming."

"I think I'll stay here."

"You'll get in trouble."

"I can't stay inside a fence forever, you know? And I want to be here when the people come."

I shook my head. "I'll have my mom invite you over for dinner on a Sunday or something. People will know there's no black bear by then. We can hang out all day. If you stay now, you'll be grounded for real."

She thought this over and then agreed.

I watched her fast-walk down Orchard Way toward her house and then tried to figure out how I was going to tell my parents.

•••

Dad was working. Mom wasn't. I had half an hour to tell her everything, and I wasn't sure how she'd react. She was in the fridge when I walked in the door. I mean, she had all the contents of the fridge on the kitchen table and she was cleaning the inside. When I walked in, I scared her.

"Oh! It's you!" she said. "You're late."

"It's me. Yeah—I got talking to a friend for a few minutes when I got off the bus."

"How was school?"

"Good," I said. "But I need to talk to you about something."

"I'm almost done here," she said. "Is everything okay?"

"Everything's great. Really great," I said.

"Help me get this stuff back in the door. I'll dry off the shelves."

We reassembled the refrigerator together and closed the door. She still had the vegetable drawers out and was washing them, and I couldn't wait to tell her so I just started.

"Some people are coming over to the house today."

"You have new friends? That's nice. Homework, though. You have to do that."

"Um—it's not really new friends. It's more official than that. I—uh—have to tell you about why I've been out at the creek so much lately."

She kept washing the drawers with her back to me. I picked up a dish towel and dried one while she washed the other one. "You pick up trash," she said. "That's what you've always done out there."

"Well, something weird happened a few weeks ago and I need to tell you about it."

She stopped washing the vegetable drawer and gave me the parental look of worry.

"Nothing bad," I said.

"So who's coming? To the house?"

"My science teacher, her biologist friend, and the game warden."

"The game warden?"

"A few weeks ago I found an animal by the creek and it's probably the weirdest animal you ever saw."

"Are they going to shoot it? Is that why the game warden is coming?"

"They're going to save it," I said. I dried the last drawer and the two of us got the veggies back inside and the fridge done.

She sat down at the kitchen table and looked at me. "Why today?"

I told her the whole story. How I found Marvin in the creek, how his family lived by the river.

"You crossed the railroad tracks," she said.

"Mom, it's really important that you don't worry about that part right now. They're coming at four thirty."

"You have to do your homework, then."

I was right. I finally told her and she didn't believe me. "Do you want to see the pictures of the animal? I have them. It eats plastic."

She laughed. "The animal eats plastic?"

I went to the computer and pulled up the cutest picture of Marvin that I could find. I figured cute would help.

"I named him Marvin," I said.

She squinted at the picture. "What is it?"

"He's a mix of things. I don't know. That's why we need a biologist."

"Your sister knew about this?"

"Oh crap," I said. "I'm going to miss her game tonight."

"Looks like I will too, now. Geez, Obe. This is all so sudden."

She started to scroll through the pictures and comment on the babies and the blue splotch on Marvin's side and I saw it was nearly four twenty.

"Mom."

"Yeah."

"I know what melted Tommy's sneakers."

She gave me the tired and worried parental look. "Oh God, Obe, please tell me it wasn't you."

"The boys stepped in Marvin's — um — just keep scrolling. You're nearly there."

She got to the scat circle pictures and said, "Oh."

"It's toxic."

"Toxic?"

"I don't know. It's not good, whatever it is. He eats plastic and then this is what he produces, and it doesn't look like it's good, does it?"

"Looks bad, all right."

"It's why they shot him with the paint, I think. Tommy said he'd kill him."

"Kill him?"

"Tommy's changed. He, like, grew up."

"Grown-ups don't go around killing things like this."

"They do if the thing melted their porch," I said.

"I really shouldn't miss Bernadette's starting game," Mom said. "But this is an emergency."

"I can handle it myself, really," I said.

"This is Devlin land. *My* land. If this animal is on *my* land, then it's *my* animal."

She had that fierce look like she did when the tree cutters and wood chippers came that first day. She had that look of one hundred years ago. No different to her grandmother, who watched the land disappear acre by acre. No different to her mother, who'd had to bury spare change in the dirt around the house. Fierce. Ready for anything.

CHAPTER 40

BIG & BIGGER

There were people who cared and people who didn't. I was the kind of person who cared. I guess this is obvious considering my habit of cleaning up other people's trash and how I treated Marvin Gardens, but sometimes I cared too much, if there was such a thing. I was the boy who'd lost his turf and buried things under people's front steps.

It was nice to meet other people who cared too much too — but it was scary. I was an eleven-year-old kid and they were professional adults who knew a lot more than I did about pretty much everything. As we waited for them to come, I got that nervous feeling and I feared a nosebleed, but then I remembered I didn't get those anymore. My hands got a little sweaty. But then I looked at Mom and I knew she was on my team. With that Devlin look in her eye.

The game warden was pretty cool. He wasn't in a uniform like I expected. He was just in jeans and a T-shirt. He stuck his hand out for me to shake and was eager to see Marvin. Ms. G introduced me to her friend, Dr. Keri. She smiled a lot and you could tell from her eyes that she was a kind person. Ms. G had changed out of her school clothes and she was in jeans and hiking boots. It was weird to see her like that.

Mom introduced herself. "I'm Kathleen Devlin," she said. Everyone shook hands and the game warden looked at me.

"Let's go see what you got, kid."

I walked them down the road instead of through *Phase Three* and said, "I really should have checked the creek first in case he's roaming for food. He usually roams after the workmen leave."

None of them answered me. I wondered if I'd even said it out loud.

When we got to the bridge, I told them to follow me and they did and I said, "Give me a little space. I don't want him to be scared."

They fell back a bit.

This was when I had all my second thoughts.

What if they took him away?

Would he end up in some lab getting shot full of weird chemicals?

Would they separate the family?

I kept walking but my feet were moving slower. I half thought about pretending that the den was somewhere else and that Marvin and his whole family were gone and there was nothing to see. *Move along! Nothing to see here!*

I stopped.

"What's wrong?" Mom asked.

"I want to make sure none of you are going to hurt Marvin."

"Who's Marvin?" the game warden said.

"It's the animal," Ms. G said.

Dr. Keri the biologist shook her head. "We're here to help. Promise."

I took a deep breath and kept walking the riverbank. The den was less than thirty feet from us now and I called out, "Hey Marvin! I'm back!"

No answer.

I walked faster.

"Marvin?"

No answer.

I ran up onto the bank and grabbed the trees to help me around the brush in front of Marvin's den. I said, "Marvin? Are you in there?"

The others stayed on the other side of the den. I got on my knees and peeked into the burrow. Marvin was there, grinning at me.

"You're real funny," I said.

Marvin made his talking noise and loped out of the den. His blue splotch was nearly gone. I looked in and saw that Boardwalk and the babies had blue paint around their lips. The paint must have been plastic. It was nice that they could eat the thing that hurt Marvin.

"I have some people I want you to meet," I said. When I turned around, the adults were looking at me like I was a little crazy.

"I talk to him to make him feel welcome here," I said. "It's not like he understands exactly what I'm saying."

The next five minutes were a mix of fast and slow. I scratched Marvin's head while the others made their way around, but there wasn't enough room for all of us.

The game warden said, "Well, I'll be damned."

Dr. Keri the biologist whispered "Wow!" maybe fifty times.

Ms. G and Mom didn't say anything. They just watched the whole thing from up a little higher on the bank.

"Maybe he's hungry," I said. "Usually he has food down here. It's all gone."

There was a splash behind me. Boardwalk was swimming.

Dr. Keri whispered "Wow" again and started taking video with a camera.

The game warden said, "This is the craziest thing I've ever seen."

Dr. Keri said, "He's so friendly."

I said, "Marvin, sit." And Marvin sat. "He's trained too. I mean, a little. I've only known him two weeks."

"You think he only started living here two weeks ago?" Dr. Keri asked.

"I don't know. It was the first time I saw him. Before that it was still cold and stuff. Maybe he came out because it's spring?" I said.

"He could hibernate, I suppose," the game warden said.

"The offspring look older than two weeks old," Dr. Keri said. "I don't think he came here to reproduce."

Boardwalk swam to the middle of the river and called out to Marvin, who was still sitting. He looked at me and then Boardwalk and he loped over to the bank and jumped into the water. He swam close to the bank until each of the babies jumped in after him. They played swimming games.

"I guess they're old enough to swim," I said.

Dr. Keri kept her video camera on the river. "I'll get DNA samples today."

"Do you have to stick him with a needle?" I asked.

"No. I can collect hair," she answered. "I'll need to get some scat too."

"Um," I said.

Ms. G said, "It's okay. I explained the scat situation."

Dr. Keri said, "I brought some metal containers in case it melts the usual specimen jars."

I looked at Ms. G and smiled, and she smiled at me. I said, "I would have never found him if I didn't collect trash in the creek."

"Obe cleans up every day. Nobody else around here does," Mom said. "He's our little conservationist."

I didn't like Mom calling me *little*. "Marvin!" I called. I held up the tennis ball. He grinned. I threw it upriver and he swam to the right place to catch it in his mouth and bring it back to shore.

"Wow," Dr. Keri whispered again.

Marvin climbed onshore, dropped the ball at my feet, and shook the water off himself. The babies and Boardwalk swam ashore after him. The five of us humans stood there, four of us in awe, and me in a state of bigness. This was my discovery, my friend, and I felt a million feet tall.

One hundred years ago, this is what it must have felt like to own 175 acres of land. Pride. One hundred years ago, it must have felt awful to lose every acre because of a *problem*. I looked at Mom standing there watching the whole Marvin family and I guessed that her fierceness came from something other than pride because her family had lost their pride. And now I knew what it was. It was shame.

I understood shame. I knew Annie understood shame. I think we both deserved to feel pride again. And so did Mom.

"So what do we do now?" I asked.

Mom looked at her watch. "We have time to make Bernadette's game if you still want to go."

Dr. Keri said, "I'll get the DNA samples. That's it for today. I'll talk with you about visiting and monitoring. I want to come back tomorrow. Same time. And I need the scat sample."

"I'm gonna have to talk to my office about what to do here," the game warden said. "I think we should get word out that this is a temporarily protected area or something. I don't know. Bears, I know what to do, but this is a new one for me."

"Why don't you take us to the scat circles, Obe?" Ms. G said. "And thank you for sharing this with us. I'm so glad you did."

And right then all four of them looked at me like I was some sort of hero, and I felt bigger than I'd ever felt.

CHAPTER 41

DEVLIN SHAME & DEVLIN PRIDE

There was protocol — a set of rules adults had to go through before they could help me and Marvin. Dr. Keri took her scat samples and the game warden said that he didn't think the pits were something to worry about. I told them about the melting sneakers and Mom gave them Tommy's mom's phone number. The game warden said, "I'll go see the residential damage now. Keri, I'll get back to you."

"Take pictures," Dr. Keri said. "I'm going to spend tomorrow looking upriver for any signs of former habitation."

I got that feeling — that feeling of getting sucker punched. "I don't want him to get hurt again before you come back. I'm really worried about him."

"I'll be back tomorrow to post some signs and maybe even tape off the area," the game warden said. "It's a good first step until we talk this over at the office."

"You're going to have to call the EPA," Dr. Keri said. She explained that the EPA is the Environmental Protection Agency. They're in charge of classifying endangered species and other things. Marvin was both a new animal who needed protection and a potential environmental risk. That's how Dr. Keri put it.

I said, "He's a slightly imperfect pollution solution."

Dr. Keri laughed.

We all agreed to meet the next day. At home, Mom started her car and I ran inside to grab my baseball cap before we went to Bernadette's game.

Mom said, "I should text your dad and tell him not to worry if there are still cars in the driveway when he gets home."

"They'll be gone by then. Don't worry about it. Let's just go see Bernadette."

"He could be very weird about all this. You know that, right?"

I said, "He'll have to believe because it's real now."

"I still can't believe it. What an amazing discovery."

"Ms. G says that Dr. Keri will write an article for a big scientific journal. We'll be famous. I mean, science famous, which I'm guessing isn't the same as TV famous, but still. I'm pretty proud to be a Devlin today."

Mom looked offended. "You aren't on other days?"

"Are you?"

"Yeah," she said.

"You didn't seem so Devlin-proud this week when you told me about not going to college and all that. I don't think you should be ashamed of what your resume looks like, anyway. You're a good person and a great mom and you work hard."

She didn't say anything for a minute. She just drove and I saw her eyes get watery. "Out of the mouths of babes," she said.

I had no idea what that meant, but I think it meant I helped her.

•••

Bernadette waved when we sat on the grass bank next to the packed bleachers. Tommy was there with his dad and I waved at him but he didn't wave back. I didn't care because I still felt bigger than the river.

They won the game, Bernadette had three hits and one run and no errors, and she was so full of pride she talked the whole way home. Mom and I didn't tell her anything about Marvin or Dr. Keri or the game warden. We just let her talk and talk and talk.

Mom's phone rang when we got into the driveway. She told us to go inside while she talked. I saw it was Tommy's mom calling. I hoped the warden didn't make her freak out or anything.

When we got inside, Bernadette went straight for the fridge and drank milk right out of the carton and said she was going to take a shower. It was still light outside and I wanted to go see Marvin, so I waited and waited for Mom to come in, but she was still in the car talking on the phone. Then the game warden's truck pulled in and I went outside.

"I'm going to get this up tonight," he said, pulling a few signs and stakes out of the back of his truck. "Wanna help me?"

Mom got out of the car. She said hello to the game warden and I told her I was going to go help him but she said, "Okay, but I want to talk to you first."

I gave her a look.

She said, "Five minutes, tops."

The game warden said, "You'll know where to find me."

Mom sat me on the back porch chair and she sat in the other one. She said, "I know what happened with Tommy."

"This isn't really important right now," I said.

"I know he punched you. I know about the turf thing."

"War."

"Yeah. Tommy's mom is thankful that you've been so quiet about what Tommy was doing. I can't say I feel the same," she said.

"Oh."

"You know to come to us if you're getting bullied or hurt or any of that. Come on. They've been teaching you this since kindergarten."

"It's different when it really happens, though," I said. "I was embarrassed."

"You didn't punch anybody."

"I got punched."

"That's nothing to be embarrassed about."

"You've obviously never been punched," I said.

She weighed it in her head. "Okay. Tommy's mom said the game warden told her to not say anything about the animal, but you know her mouth, right? You know that by the weekend, everyone here will know what's going on."

"There's about to be a big fence around the whole area," I said. "People will know by tomorrow morning."

"Exactly. Just be careful, okay? Out there by the river, in school, on the bus, just be careful," she said.

I thought back to Annie running right toward the train tracks that afternoon. "I'm always careful."

"I'm really proud of you. For all of this. For making it through. For all you put up with and for dealing with Tommy the way you did—though I really wish you would have told us."

"Did Tommy's mom talk at all about his sister?"

"No."

"She pulled her car up to me the other day and called me a little jerk."

Mom raised an eyebrow.

I said, "And I saw a text on Bernadette's phone from her too. It was really mean. Something about getting Bernadette kicked off the team."

"Thank you for telling me this," Mom said—the Devlin fierceness back in her eyes. "Now go. Have some fun."

CHAPTER 42

TALKING & TALKING

There were rules now. No one could go down to the river. No one could play in the woods. I was allowed to walk to the creek and clean it up if I wanted, but I couldn't pass the tree line unless the warden was there.

There were rule-breakers. Only one, maybe. It was me.

I got up at five in the morning

I didn't have to sneak out of the house but I wasn't loud about it. I walked right down the road and onto the riverbank and right to Marvin's den and it was empty.

I made a few of the talking noises that Marvin made. I heard splashing and looked downriver and there they were — the family of Marvins in the dawn light having a swim. Marvin came to the bank and climbed up and sat down on my foot, which soaked my sneaker but I didn't care.

I sat down cross-legged and talked to him.

"We're making sure you're safe," I said. "Everyone is going to know about you soon. It could get weird. I don't want people coming here and taking pictures of you or anything like that. They're all supposed to stay away."

Marvin nudged me because he knew I had plastic bags in my pockets. I handed him one and he gnawed on it.

"I don't know, Marvin. You're so different and weird and some people might not like you," I said. "I guess we have a lot in common."

He nudged me for another plastic bag. Boardwalk and the babies were up on the bank now, walking toward the den.

"Dr. Keri said you might have come from upriver," I said, and pointed upriver. Marvin grinned. I knew he didn't understand a word I was saying. "And if you did, then maybe you'll be moving downriver soon. That's my guess. If I could swim downriver, I might do it. I've always wanted to be nomadic. You know in less than a hundred miles you'll be all the way to Philadelphia. I bet you'll find a lot more plastic to eat near a city."

Boardwalk and the babies sat around me. I was part of their family. Something was different. I didn't know what it was.

We watched the sun rise upstream while we sat next to the river. It was the most beautiful sunrise I ever saw. I rubbed the babies' slimy tummies and I thought about Tommy.

"You really helped me, Marvin," I said. "These last few years have been so hard with all these new people in my field. Remember my story about the field? About how we used to own all this land?"

Marvin put his snout into my pocket and got the rest of the bags. He gave them to Boardwalk.

"Anyway, thank you. I have to go and get ready for school, okay?"

He grinned that dumb grin.

"And don't be afraid if Dr. Keri comes around today. She's a smart lady. I have to go to school, otherwise I'd stay here with you all day."

I rubbed all the slimy bellies one more time and then got up and walked back toward the road.

CHAPTER 43

TOMMY & OLD SNEAKERS

There were notes. One was on my bed when I came back from seeing Marvin that morning. It was from Mom. One was slipped into my backpack at the bus stop. It was from Tommy.

Mom's note said: *I didn't tell your dad anything last night. I'm telling him today when the game warden comes back. We both have the day off. We'll see you when you get home!*

Tommy's note said: *I'm really sorry for punching you and starting the turf war. My mom told me I should thank you for not saying anything about it so I guess thanks. I don't really like these other kids that much. I thought you should know that. And please tell Annie I'm sorry about kissing her.*

On the way to school, Annie chatting in my ear the whole way about how I was going to be famous, I thought about loners. Marvin was a loner — even with his family, he was still on his own, I was a loner. My dad was a loner and my mom was too. Even though they were married, they were married loners. Annie was a loner because people called her putrid and because of her backyard play prison. Even Tommy was a loner because he was stuck with a bunch of boys he didn't like but hung out with anyway. We were all loners because we felt like we had to do what someone else told us to do.

I wondered when we would just be able to do what felt right. I wondered when we'd be able to be ourselves and not be called names. I wondered when we could wear old sneakers. Middle school was coming. Dances and awkward stuff I didn't want to think about. I wanted to be eleven forever, but I knew how time worked.

One hundred years ago, time moved at the exact same pace. One hundred years ago, boys grew up and girls grew up and nothing much had changed except now we played video games when we used to play and work outside, I guess.

Annie was still talking. I felt bad for not listening. I was having a different kind of day. A big day. The last thing I heard her say was, "Okay? I'll see you then."

I looked at her and tried to understand when she'd see me. Or where. I felt like the worst friend in the world right then. I should have told her about Marvin the day I found him. But then again, we were all loners.

We got off the bus and I headed to Ms. G's room to tell her that I saw Marvin that morning.

"Hey Obe!" Tommy yelled from behind me. "Wait up!"

227

I waited. "Oh hi," I said.

"Did you read my note?"

"Yeah. Thanks."

"Did you tell Annie I'm sorry?"

"No," I said. "You're going to have to do that yourself."

"Oh," he said. "I guess."

I wanted to tell him I missed him but I couldn't. Not because Dad told me that boys aren't supposed to have feelings. Not because he'd once sucker punched me in the nose. But because I wasn't sure if I missed him.

"Can we hang out this weekend?" he asked.

"Really?"

"My mom told me about Marvin," he said. "I mean, she doesn't know that's his name, but you know what I mean."

"We're not allowed anywhere near him," I said. "The game warden has it all cordoned off."

"I saw you down there this morning," he said. "Anyway, I don't want to see Marvin. I want to go burying things. Like the old days."

I thought about how my things were buried all over the developments and it made me sad. I wished I could dig them all up.

"I don't want to bury things anymore," I said.

Tommy looked at me weird and I looked at him weird. Neither of us knew what had happened to us. Maybe he tried to grow up by wearing the right kind of sneakers and failed. Maybe I didn't try to grow up but accidentally did by enduring everything I'd gone through since he'd sucker punched me in the nose. And by finding Marvin Gardens.

"I'll come over after lunch one day," he said. When he walked away I saw he was wearing a new pair of sneakers. Not the fancy kind. The kind he always used to wear.

I poked my head into Ms. G's room and saw other kids there—her homeroom kids—and I walked in and said, "Thank you for Dr. Keri and everything."

"Thank you for Marvin Gardens."

"Pretty amazing, right?" I asked.

"Pretty amazing," she said.

I didn't know Tommy was still behind me. When I turned around he said, "Dude, she just winked at you," like he was jealous.

"I've been working on my contest project with her is all," I said.

"But she winked!"

How could anyone have a crush on a teacher? It was so weird. But she did wink. And it did make me smile. I didn't have a crush on her, but I hoped that when I was thirty and she was in her eighties we could sometimes meet and eat lunch together or something.

Not a typical loner thought, but maybe I wasn't meant to be a loner forever.

CHAPTER 44

ONE HUNDRED YEARS AGO

One hundred years ago or so, my great-grandfather and great-grandmother moved their family from the big farmhouse to the little one — the one we live in now. It was the only thing they had left of the farm. The only thing they had left, period. My great-grandfather couldn't afford to have a *problem* anymore and he went teetotal. That's what they called not drinking anymore. There was no more dirt to drink.

One hundred years ago, it wasn't perfect. Nothing was ever perfect, probably. I bet even back when dinosaurs were around, things weren't perfect.

My great-grandparents lived out the rest of their years in this house. They had a big garden and they lived small. Their kids helped them out when they could. My great-grandfather died before my mom was born, from the complications of drinking dirt. His liver finally gave out because being teetotal didn't turn back time. My great-grandmother turned to chickens. She filled the yard with them——all different breeds. She started showing them and winning prizes. She had fun. My mom says it might have been the first time in her grandmother's adult life that she had fun. Two years after her husband died, she sold enough fancy chickens to make $600. That's how she bought back that little slice of land with Devlin Creek on it——the wild patch. It didn't cost her much. But it meant the world.

CHAPTER 45

PIZZA & CREEK TIME

There was science. Dr. Keri said maybe Marvin could help in the development of a new plastic — one that broke down faster. "Maybe if we can find a type of plastic that makes his scat less toxic, we can find a type of plastic that's less harmful to all of us," she said.

The game warden and Dr. Keri came by on Friday night and filled us in on how things were going for Marvin. Dad looked oddly comfortable with the whole thing. Mom must have shown him the pictures or maybe he was just keeping up appearances around the game warden. I couldn't tell. I didn't care. He was one kind of person and I was another kind. I still loved him. He was my dad.

Dr. Keri had found scat circles twenty miles upriver thanks to a game warden in the neighboring county who'd noticed them after some hunters lost the soles of their boots to it.

"I think he's nomadic," I said.

"I plan on following him," Dr. Keri said. "This is kind of a biologist's dream, you know."

"For now, he's here and he's my responsibility," the game warden said. "I have signs up and I've talked to the construction company. They're giving us a week."

"A week to do what?" I asked.

"A week to protect the area or not," he said. "But you can't get an animal protected in a week. Just doesn't work that way. Government organizations are slower than anything you can ever imagine with stuff like this."

Dr. Keri huffed out her nose and smirked. "This is why I hope they *are* nomadic. It's easier than sitting around waiting for the government."

When they left, Dad ordered a pizza and the four of us sat down to eat.

"I'm proud of you, Obe," Dad said.

"Thanks," I said.

"Bernadette, you had a great week. Proud of you too."

Bernadette looked at all of us like this was the weirdest thing ever, and it was, kind of, so I didn't blame her.

"I talked to Tommy's mother again today," Mom said. "Bernadette, tell me if that daughter of hers gives you any more trouble."

Bernadette looked at me. I shrugged. "Okay, Mom," she said.

"Do you guys want to come out to the creek with me tonight?" I asked. "Could be fun. It's warm enough to dip our feet in."

"The mosquitoes," Mom said. "I'll get eaten alive."

"Bug spray, Mom. It's easy now. You just spray it on," I said.

"I haven't been out there in a while," Dad said. "Come on, Kath. It'll be fun."

Bernadette didn't say much, but she nodded. She was eating two slices of pizza at the same time like a pizza sandwich because her coach said that the next week was going to be hard training.

After dinner, the creek was quiet. I walked to halfway across my log bridge and sat down.

"I bet there's hundreds of crayfish in there," Bernadette said.

"Remember catching the granddaddy that time?" Dad said. "Man, was he huge."

"He pinched my finger," Bernadette said. "I cried for an hour."

"I wish Marvin would come up to meet you, Dad. You'd like him."

"Who's Marvin?"

"It's what he named the animal," Mom said.

"Marvin Gardens," Bernadette said.

"Hey! That's a cool name!" Dad said, not realizing any irony ever.

"God, this creek is beautiful," Mom said. "Even with all those houses in the background."

I smiled.

She said, "I bet we could plant the property line with trees — those tall bushes even. What are those called? Anyway, we could block off the developments so we wouldn't have to see them."

"Wouldn't block the barking dogs or the bulldozers," Bernadette said.

"Bulldozers will be gone once this part's done," Dad said. "And the dogs we'll just have to get used to."

"It's almost an acre between here and the house. I was thinking about planting a vegetable garden and some flowers or something," I said.

"I think it would look great," Mom said. "My grandmother bought this back after Granddad died. Just so we could have the creek. She'd like it if we made it pretty."

"We could make it like a little private park or something," Bernadette said. "I always wanted a hammock."

Mom laughed at that. I knew what she was thinking because I'd heard her say it enough times. She grew up on a farm, far away from hammocks and private parks. Land wasn't for those things. Until now. Her face was soft about it, like she was changing right there by the creek. And then she slapped her leg hard and swore under her breath about the mosquitoes.

This was the end of creek time. Dad already had his back turned to the creek and was standing, looking at our house.

"I don't get enough time outside," he said. "I don't appreciate this place as much as I should."

None of us said anything. I wanted to, but I figured Dad might realize a lot of things if he came outside more.

CHAPTER 46

SUNRISES & SIGNS

There were early mornings I liked and early mornings I didn't like. Five o'clock on a Saturday morning wasn't my idea of a good early morning. Something woke me but I didn't know what it was. I decided to get up.

There was no traffic on a Saturday morning at five. Not one car passed me on my way down the road toward the river.

I heard splashing in the river and couldn't quite see the path in front of me, but I walked fast. Marvin called out with a wail. *That was what woke me up,* I thought.

As I neared the den, I saw Marvin had moved things. The cover was gone — the brush was all clear and the path wasn't broken anymore by the sticks and brambles he'd put there to camouflage his house. There were no random plastic snacks. It was as if he'd never lived there, really, if you didn't look too hard.

All six of the Marvins were out in the river swimming. Floating, really. Boardwalk was on her back and the babies were lounging on her belly.

Marvin called out to me.

I waved. I looked around the den for the tennis ball, but it wasn't there either.

They started swimming with the current. Not swimming hard, but a mix of floating and treading. I thought Marvin would circle back, and yet I knew he wasn't coming back. I knew he was on his way to the next place.

So I just stood there on the bank of the river and watched them float away. The sun rose behind me, and as the river turned, I lost sight of them. I sat down next to the abandoned den and cried. I wasn't sad. I was happy. Happy Marvin would get away from whoever shot him with a paintball. Happy that Dr. Keri would follow him and write about him and protect him along the way. Happy that I'd had my time with him.

It was the perfect ending, really. One hundred years from now, how many people would come to this part of the river and know that an entire species was discovered right here? One hundred years from now, how many other plastic-eating species would there be? Would everyone recycle? Would people live a different way—a way that helped the planet? Would the Great Pacific Garbage Patch shrink? Would someone invent a way to clean the air and the water and the soil? A lot can happen in one hundred years. Maybe if everyone realized that we could change the world, we'd learn to live differently.

I blew my nose in my sweatshirt and even though I was cauterized, I still looked for blood but there wasn't any. I got up and started walking back to the house. When I got halfway up the road, I decided to go to the creek for a while.

Phase Three was the same as I left it the last time I was there. On its way to building eight *New Spacious Homes!* on Drowning House Road. It didn't make me too sad anymore. Can't stop time.

I passed through the tree line and went to walk across my log bridge, but the rising sun reflected off something weird. I got closer and saw what it was. It was six of my Matchbox cars — the ones I'd buried in *Phase Three* — lined up on the log. My first thought was that someone else had done this. Tommy. Bernadette. Anyone. But no one knew where I'd buried those cars. I'd buried them with Marvin.

Something about it made me know that everything was going to be okay. Something about it made me know I'd see Marvin again too.

•••

Tommy came to our door while I was trying to clean my room. Saturday chores. Mom must have let him in, and the next thing I knew he was lying on my bedroom floor, paging through my animal track guide.

"What species do you think he is?"

"Mammal."

"I mean, is he a pig or a dog or a cat or what? I can't remember his face."

"His face was like a tapir and an aardvark and a hog all mixed together," I said.

"Do you have any drawings of his tracks? Or will we go find some fresh ones today and get molds?"

"He left this morning," I said. "He's nomadic—a migrant species, we think."

Tommy didn't say anything for a while. Then he said, "So what do you want to do today?"

I stopped cleaning my room. It was hopeless. "I want to clear out all the weeds in the wild patch. My dad said we'd make it a really pretty place. Block off the view of Phase Three. Plant some trees. So I'll start by clearing what's there."

"I'm in."

I still didn't really trust Tommy. But I thought of Marvin and how he trusted humans when he really shouldn't, so I trusted Tommy anyway—at least for today.

CHAPTER 47

WINNERS & LOSERS

There were newspaper stories. There were visits from Dr. Keri. There were e-mailed pictures of Marvin and Boardwalk's new home downriver. The babies were growing.

There was a picture of me standing next to Marvin — one that Dr. Keri took on that first day — surrounded by newspaper clippings in the glass display case right when you walked into our school. It made me self-conscious, but Tommy said it should make me feel cool.

There was Annie Bell, who stayed in seat twelve with me and showed me her rocks and talked to me about El Niño and the Farmer's Almanac's predictions for summer. When we'd hang out at the creek, she'd pull more rocks from the creek bed and we'd walk the railroad tracks and look for old train marbles when my mom and dad weren't around to tell us not to be fearless, daring, and brave. Tommy stayed with his new friends and they treated him better even though he wore cheap sneakers. Mike said that he wanted to be friends with me too, but I decided to wait and make my mind up after summer.

There was the science contest. I won it with my project about a brand-new animal. An animal that ate plastic. An animal whose scat could eat a hole in your shoes or your floor or your car tire. I called the project THE SLIGHTLY IMPERFECT POLLUTION SOLUTION. I figured there was no point in lying since none of us were perfect. I used some of Dr. Keri's videos. I used my original pictures. I wrote a research paper that was three times as long as anyone else's.

There would be a summer vacation working with Dr. Keri sometimes and playing with Marvin as he moved downriver. There would be more games of fetch and more research and more conservation and more conversation about how Marvin could help us and how we could help him. It was a long process. That's all anyone ever said about conservation. *It's a long process.* I was happy I got to be part of it, no matter how long it would be.

There was a future in this. Ms. G said I'd make a great scientist. She said I could do what Dr. Keri did or I could be one of those people who travels the world helping animals in places where habitats were being destroyed. She told me I could be on TV if I wanted. I could be anything I wanted to be. But really, I knew I wanted to be a teacher like her. Finding Marvin Gardens had taught me so much. I wanted to pass it on.

One hundred years ago, science teachers were explaining to students how the Wright brothers flew an airplane in Kitty Hawk, North Carolina, in 1903. One hundred years ago, science teachers were talking about Albert Einstein's theory of relativity. One hundred years from now, teachers would be teaching about things we would never guess. I wanted to do that. I wanted to find other kids like me and make them care about where they lived and how to make things better.

One hundred years ago, my great-grandmother had a dream. I like to think she dreamed of a day her great-grandson won a science contest and decided to become a teacher. I like to think she dreamed of the day her wild patch, the only piece of her own dirt she could buy back, would thrive and hold her family close.

And it did.

We planted a garden and fruit trees and wildflowers. We picnicked there. We had campfires there. We even pitched a tent in summer sometimes and slept there. Bernadette brought her boyfriends there (but don't tell Dad), and one day I would sit at the picnic table beside the creek and fill out my college applications there.

I would read my acceptance letters.

I would read my rejection letters too.

I would write my graduation speech about the day I found an

animal and thought he was eating my liver. The speech would be about the nature of fear and how it stops us from doing things.

There was hope. There had to be hope.

A Devlin with purpose couldn't be discouraged.

And I wasn't.

ACKNOWLEDGMENTS

I owe thanks to many people. First, Michael Bourret, for being the best agent in the world; Cheryl Klein, whose hand guided mine as I wrote; and the entire team at Arthur A. Levine Books, who made this book possible. Thank you to Sy Montgomery, who gave me perfect advice, and to the real Ms. G, who inspired me to always look for more meaning in the world. I could never find meaning in the destruction of my perfect cornfield until I wrote this book; now I know every adventure I've lived was because I witnessed its demolition.

Sometimes life is weird like that. Bad turns into good. Kind of like recycling.

ABOUT THE AUTHOR

Amy Sarig King, who also writes as A.S. King, grew up in the middle of a cornfield in southeastern Pennsylvania. She says, "The day the bulldozers came to dig up my field was the day I started to dream of having my own farm. If you've ever seen something beautiful and magical be replaced with something more convenient, then you know why this story took me thirty years to write."

Amy has published many critically acclaimed young adult novels, including *Please Ignore Vera Dietz*, which was named a Michael L. Printz Honor Book, and *Ask the Passengers*, which won the Los Angeles Times Book Prize. After many years farming abroad, she now lives back in southeastern Pennsylvania, with her family. Visit her website at www.as-king.com and follow her on Twitter at @AS_King.

"...somewhere nice."